Double or Nothing

Double or Nothing

Nancy Baker Jacobs

Five Star • Waterville, Maine

Five Star First Edition Mystery Series.

Published in 2001in conjunction with Tekno-Books and Ed Gorman.

Set in 11 pt. Plantin by Myrna S. Raven.

Printed in the United States on permanent paper.

Library of Congress Cataloging-in-Publication Data

Jacobs, Nancy Baker, 1944–
    Double or nothing / Nancy Baker Jacobs.
        p.   cm.—(Five Star first edition mystery series)
    ISBN 0-7862-3010-X (hc : alk. paper)
    1. San Francisco (Calif.)—Fiction. 2. Home exchanging
—Fiction. 3. Kidnapping—Fiction. 4. Sisters—Fiction.
I. Title. II. Series.
PS3560.A2554 D68 2001
    813′.54—dc21   2001040106

Double or Nothing

1

Herb Carmody stood on the balcony of his wife's hilltop house, holding a glass of single malt Scotch and staring wistfully across the bay at the San Francisco skyline. If only he could disappear into that horizon, he thought as he watched the sunset turn the top floors of the Bank of America building and the pyramid-shaped Transamerica tower from pink to purple and finally to gray. If only he could hide in the depths of the city across the water, somewhere neither Jane nor Kozlowski would ever find him, someplace where he could make a fresh start.

As he sipped his Scotch, the white lights along the graceful lines of the Bay Bridge blinked on for the evening. Every time he stood in this spot, gazing toward the southern sky, Herb's art lover's eye was struck anew by the juxtaposition of nature's physical beauty with some of man's greatest feats of engineering. He couldn't help being impressed by the famed bridges spanning the brilliant blue waters of San Francisco Bay; the skyscrapers delicately perched on the city's famous hilly terrain; the massive ships steaming toward one of the world's great harbors; the shiny silver jumbo jets taking off and landing at San Francisco International Airport. As darkness began to fall and the colors of the Bay deepened and changed, the twinkling lights in the distance lent an ethereal quality to the panoramic view. No wonder Jane had fallen in love with this house, Herb thought in a moment of understanding. If his wife had bothered to consult him before she bought it, no doubt he would have applauded her taste.

The telephone rang once, then a second time. Irritated by

the interruption of his reverie, Herb stepped into the house and grabbed the portable phone off the end of the bar. "Hello."

"Late again, Carmody."

As he recognized the raspy male voice on the other end of the line, Herb's hand jerked and several drops of the Scotch he was holding slopped over the side of the glass onto the ivory carpet. "How'd you get this number?" He eyed the hallway nervously, but he was in luck; Jane was nowhere in sight.

"I got ways. Listen, asshole, I'm real close to losin' patience. Your tab's up another five grand after yesterday. Now you miss this morning's payment. Not smart."

Herb hurried back outside, set his drink on the balcony railing, and slid the glass door closed behind him. He couldn't chance Jane's overhearing this conversation, not unless he wanted to be out of here on his ass. "Hey, Kozlowski, give me a break. How was I s'posed to know the Athletics would lose three in a row? Shit, they finally had the home field advantage. They should've won easy."

"I'm all teary-eyed. That's the concept, idiot. Somebody wins, somebody loses. You pick Oakland over Anaheim yesterday, you lose. And you been losin' enough lately to make me real nervous. Tab's pushin' a hundred grand and I'm cuttin' you off. Time to pay up."

"Yeah, sure, I know. I'm working on it. You'll get your money. It's not like I'm trying to welsh on—"

"Welshin' on Kozlowski ain't an option."

Herb began to shiver in the cool night air. "Sure, sure, I hear you. Listen, I got ten grand set aside for you in the safe at the gallery, like I promised," he said. "Couldn't get it over to you today, that's all. But first thing tomorrow—"

"Give ya till noon."

"Deal. But listen. You can't call me at home again, Kozlowski."

"Next time, I ain't gonna be callin' you, Carmody. You don't get the message, next time I call that rich little wife of yours, see if she hears better'n you. Get me that ten by noon tomorrow and fifteen more by the end of the week. Then it'll be twenty-five a week till you're paid up."

"But I can't poss—" The dial tone buzzed in Herb's ear; Kozlowski had hung up. "Son of a bitch!" Herb muttered under his breath. There was no way he could come up with twenty-five grand a week. Once, maybe, he could siphon off that kind of money without Jane's finding out. But not four weeks in a row. He switched off the phone and gulped down the rest of his Scotch. As he started back inside the house, he glanced briefly to his left and caught a glimpse of the only nearby neighbor on the exclusive hilltop. He could see a glint of light reflecting against the old woman's thick eyeglasses as she spied on him through a slit in her living room drapes. He raised his glass in a mock toast and the drapes quickly closed again.

"Nosy old bitch," Herb muttered under his breath. Had Louise Justman overheard his phone conversation? No, he told himself, that was crazy, sheer paranoia. And, even if she had, who could she tell about it? The old woman had never exchanged two words with either him or Jane, and she never left her house. The real estate agent who'd sold Jane the house said that the reclusive Mrs. Justman had been a widow for years and that she had anything and everything she needed delivered. As far as Herb could tell, her only hobby seemed to be spying on her new neighbors, although that seemed to keep her pretty damned busy. Neighborhood Watch for the wealthy elite, Herb thought.

When the telephone rang, Jane Carmody was sitting at her

dressing table in the master bedroom, brushing her long, curly mop of red hair into place. She ignored the phone. Herb was already dressed; he could answer it.

Jane always required longer to make herself presentable than her husband did, to prepare herself physically and mentally for a social occasion. She especially needed more time to get ready for an event as important as tonight's, when she was scheduled to introduce the charity dinner's guest speaker.

She picked up an emerald-and-pearl hair ornament that matched her earrings and necklace. Pulling her hair away from her face, she positioned the ornament to hold the bright red mass in place behind her left ear. Checking her reflection in the mirror, she shuddered slightly. For an instant, she saw a skinny fifteen-year-old playing dress-up, a pale, freckled girl with a face cursed by her father's enormous nose. The familiar taunt, "Hey, bird beak!" echoed painfully in her ears. "Hey, pelican puss, wanna fish?" For years, she'd been called pelican or stork—it always seemed to be some sort of bird reference—and the taunts had only gotten worse her senior year of high school, when a fall had put her on crutches for six months. Jane still carried deep scars from those hated nicknames of her youth. *That's not you,* she lectured herself, shaking her hairbrush at her reflected image. *That's not you anymore.* She squeezed her eyes as tightly closed as she could without smearing her fresh mascara. Following her therapist's teaching, she took a deep breath and forced her neck and shoulder muscles to go limp for a few seconds while she silently repeated her mantra. When she reopened her eyes, the scrawny fifteen-year-old in the mirror had disappeared. In her place now was a woman much closer to reality—a pretty woman whose appearance was the result of another fifteen years' maturity, two years of physical therapy to eradicate her limp, and a new nose sculpted by a masterful plastic surgeon. She was dressed in an elegant emerald silk gown that matched her eyes and complemented her fiery hair.

That's more like it, Jane thought as she continued her mental pep talk. People at tonight's fund-raiser might stare at her, but it wouldn't be because she was a freak, not anymore. It would be because she had an important spot on the program, maybe even because she was attractive. She'd changed drastically since she was a girl, was still changing daily. What she needed to do now was forget about miserable, self-conscious young Jane Parkhurst, make herself remember that she was Jane Carmody, Mrs. Herbert Carmody, respectable California socialite who had no reason to feel second best to anybody.

Still seated at the mirror, Jane practiced the short introduction she'd prepared for tonight. She rattled off the speaker's resume, then added a few more personal words: "I'm particularly delighted to introduce tonight's speaker because, to me, he's much more than one of America's leading researchers in orthopedics. The truth is, without him, I probably couldn't walk up to this podium and speak to you tonight. Fifteen years ago, I was thrown from a horse and trampled. My leg was crushed. This man was my surgeon and I'll always be grateful. Now I hope that, because of fund-raisers like tonight's, every child who comes to Children's Orthopedic Hospital will have the same chance for full recovery I had. So it's a special honor for me to present tonight's keynote speaker—Dr. William Perlmutter." She smiled broadly and practiced gesturing toward her left, where she'd been told Dr. Perlmutter would be seated.

Not bad, Jane decided, assessing her rehearsal. She would do all right as long as she kept her mind focused on the goal— tonight's hundred-dollar-a-plate dinner would raise more than thirty thousand dollars for the hospital's research projects—and stopped obsessing about screwing up Dr. Perlmutter's introduction or making a fool of herself in a dozen other ways.

Jane slid her chair backward and stood up. She glanced one last time in the mirror, gave herself a quick nod of approval, and crossed the bedroom to her dresser. She opened the top drawer, took out the checkbook with the tooled leather cover, and wrote a check for five thousand dollars to the Children's Orthopedic Hospital Auxiliary. The hospital was her pet charity and she could afford to support it generously. After she signed the check, she ripped it from the book and opened the check register to record it.

The balance in the joint account was just under fourteen thousand dollars, Jane noticed, plenty to cover tonight's donation with a comfortable margin. But as she started to enter check number 523, she realized that a check was missing. The last one recorded in the register was number 521. She'd written it herself last Friday to pay the dressmaker who'd altered tonight's dress for her. Where was check number 522? She picked up the one she'd just written. It was number 523, all right. And no checks had been entered into the register out of numerical order. Had she written another check over the weekend and forgotten to record it? Jane searched her memory and decided she had not.

Herbert, she thought with a sinking feeling. *Herbert's done it again.* She felt a slight wave of nausea. This was happening too often lately, much too often. Jane slipped on her gold high-heeled shoes, picked up the checkbook, and headed for the living room.

Jane was his real problem, Herb decided as he refilled his glass at the bar. If only everything around him didn't belong to his increasingly tight-fisted wife, he wouldn't have these terrible financial problems, he could pay off Kozlowski in a second . . . but it did belong to her. This house was Jane's, bought with her inheritance from her father; Herb's name wasn't even on the deed. He'd seen it, though, chafing as he read the words that vested the title in "Jane Parkhurst Carmody, a married woman, as her separate property." Inherited money was the only kind not considered community property under California law. And Jane's wealth was one hundred percent inherited.

That was bad enough, but what really pissed off Herb was that both of his marine art galleries—Waves and Waves II— remained legally half Jane's, despite the fact that he'd long ago repaid her father every cent he'd borrowed to buy them. That bundle he'd made on his World Series bet a few years back had retired the last of Herb's debt to the Parkhursts. If only he still had that kind of luck, he thought. Even with the economy doing so well these days, his galleries weren't taking in much more than enough to cover the employee payroll. Rich people were putting their money in the stock market or Internet startups, not marine art. And now his recent bets had all turned sour.

The way things were right now, Herb knew he was trapped between Kozlowski's goon squad and Jane Parkhurst Carmody. His wife had all the money and it just wasn't fair. She owned him, body and soul. If leaving her wouldn't break him financially, Herb knew he wouldn't be standing here right now, in this stupid monkey suit with its too-tight cumberbund, on his way to another charity fund-raiser with those snooty socialites Jane was always kissing up to. If only he had his own money, he'd be freed of the constant play-acting his marriage to a rich woman he didn't love required. He could see himself now—driving up the Coast Highway in a shiny red Ferrari with the salt-laced wind blowing through his dark blond hair—a completely free man.

Herb poured himself another scant shot of Scotch at the bar. Ignoring the silver ice tongs, he reached into the antique silver ice bucket and picked out an ice cube, plopped it into his cut glass tumbler, and used his finger to swirl it around in the amber liquid.

"Who called?"

Herb swiveled around and saw Jane standing in the arch of the living room door. She looked spectacular tonight, he had to give her that much—a vision in tones of vibrant emerald and russet and creamy ivory. She'd changed for the better in the year since her father died—physically, at least. Too bad she hadn't thrown off her father's philosophy about money the way she had the Parkhurst nose. "What?" he said.

"I heard the telephone ring. Who called?"

"Uh— Wrong number." Herb gulped his drink.

"Better go easy on that stuff, Herb. We've got a long night ahead of us."

Herb obediently set the glass down on the bar. "New dress?" he asked.

"I wanted to look good tonight. This party's important to me."

Herb nodded his agreement, although the last thing he felt like doing tonight was sitting around with a bunch of self-satisfied rich bitches telling themselves how worthy they were for donating big bucks to "those poor little crippled children." All Herb wanted from that segment of society was their envy. He wanted the opportunity to snub these stuck-up snobs the way their kind had always snubbed him. "You look spectacular tonight, Jane," he said, forcing a smile onto his lips. "You don't have to worry; you'll make just the right impression on San Francisco's upper crust."

Jane noticed the sarcastic edge in her husband's voice and

didn't return his smile. "You wrote another check on my account," she said.

For the first time, Herb noticed that Jane was holding something in her hand. He swallowed hard as he recognized the First Federal checkbook with the tooled brown leather cover.

"What check?"

"There's a check missing and it's not listed in the register. I noticed it when I made out my donation for the hospital. I haven't written any checks since Friday, so it has to be you."

Herb picked up his glass and took another gulp of Scotch, hoping it would give him courage, but it hit his stomach like acid. "Oh, right, that check," he answered, his mind searching feverishly for an acceptable excuse. "Didn't I enter it in the register? Damn, sure thought I did."

"I'll do it right now," Jane said, clicking her pen into writing position. She had an uneasy feeling. She'd played this scene before. "Who'd you write it to, and for how much?"

Herb stiffened his spine. He'd known there would be a confrontation like this; there always was, sooner or later. But he hadn't thought Jane would find out about that check quite this fast. He'd bet on having another week or two before the monthly bank statement showed up. By then, he'd hoped to make a few good wagers and replace the money. Obviously, he'd bet wrong. Again. "Cash," he said. "For, uh, ten."

"Ten dollars?"

Herb stared at the floor and mumbled, "Ten thousand."

"Ten thousand dollars?" Jane's voice rose in shock and anger. She could tell by the guilty look on Herb's face that she'd heard right. "My God, what made you think you could just take ten thousand dollars out of my checking account without asking me?"

"Calm down, Jane," Herb said, trying to gain the offen-

15

sive. "It's not *your* checking account. It's *ours,* and I needed that cash to make the payroll for the galleries. Receipts have been down this month, that's all." That wasn't entirely true, of course. The galleries' earnings were down, but he needed that ten grand to pacify Kozlowski for a few more days. By the end of the week, he'd need another fifteen. He certainly couldn't admit that to Jane, though. She'd never even heard of Kozlowski and Herb intended to keep it that way. His very existence depended upon keeping it that way. Herb knew Jane and her strong feelings about what was right and what was wrong far too well to confide in her about this kind of thing, to risk throwing himself on her mercy and begging for the money to get Kozlowski off his back. If he did that, she'd probably divorce him on the spot for deceiving her, and then he'd really be penniless. Or worse yet, she might well decide that turning Kozlowski in to the cops would solve the problem. Herb winced, just thinking about how fast Kozlowski would have his balls in the grinder if—

"Maybe your name's printed on these checks right along with mine, but there's none of your money in this account, is there?" Jane marched toward her husband, holding the checkbook out in front of her like a stiletto. When he didn't answer her, didn't even seem to be listening to her, her sense of having been wronged boiled over and she poked him hard in the stomach with the stiff leather cover.

Herb grabbed Jane's hand and pushed it away from his mid-section, then let her go. "Hey, watch it!"

"What are you trying to do to me?" Jane demanded. "Last month it was eight thousand, the month before it was five. Now ten. Damn it! The check I just wrote to the Hospital Auxiliary's going to bounce and—" Her knuckles were white against the golden brown of the checkbook cover.

Herb brought himself back to the present. "Don't be silly,

sweetheart." He forced a conciliatory tone into his voice. "Your check's not going to bounce. We'll just transfer over some money from one of your other accounts in the morning."

Jane's shoulders sagged as though she were carrying a heavy weight. Well, she was, she thought. She just couldn't figure out why. "This your way of telling me you've got somebody else?" she asked.

"What do you mean, somebody else?"

"Another woman."

"You've got to be—" Herb's face registered shock, hurt. "For chrissakes Jane, whatever gave you the idea—"

"*The money,* Herb, all that money you've been stealing from me lately. What in the hell are you spending so much money on if it's not some other woman? I mean, I'm not stupid. It's obviously not cars or clothes—I'd be able to see that. And I don't think it's dope—it's not, is it?"

"Give me a break! First you call me a thief, and now I'm a drug addict and a womanizer, too!" Herb grasped Jane by her bare shoulders and forced her to look him straight in the eye. "Listen to me carefully—I needed the ten grand for the business payroll, and I'll put the money back as soon as I can. It's that simple."

"Don't lie to me. *Please.*" Jane wrenched her shoulders away and tossed the checkbook onto the bar. It skidded across the marble surface and came to a stop against the Scotch bottle. Exactly when had things changed between them? Where had they started to go so wrong? "I—I just can't take much more of this. You—you've gotten so—so two-faced, sneaking around behind my back all the time. I just don't know what to believe anymore. You act like I shouldn't even question all the crap you've been pulling on me, like you think I owe you something, or you're doing me a big hairy

17

favor to stay married to me."

"That's ridiculous. I love you, you know that."

"Then why do you keep doing this to me, over and over and over again?"

Herb didn't reply. He reached over and picked his glass up off the bar and, the more cornered he felt, the more tightly he gripped it. He felt like an adolescent again, listening to his mother lecture him about treating her fat cat boss and his family nice or the two of them would be thrown off the estate. "You want to live in the streets, Herbie?" his mother would ask. "You want us to end up on welfare? That what you want? You listen to me—you better lose that rotten attitude and quit actin' like everybody owes you, or that's right where you're gonna end up!"

"Sometimes I think the only thing you really love is money," Jane said.

As he recalled his mother's all-too-similar words, and saw his wife's self-pitying expression, Herb's rage simmered. Right now, he saw Jane as a symbol of everyone who'd ever put him down, of all the people who'd crapped on him in the past because he was Mamie Carmody's little bastard. It cost him every scrap of his self-control not to toss what was left of the Scotch straight into his wife's face. Hell, he thought, it would practically be self-defense, wouldn't it? He imagined Jane wincing at the sting of alcohol in her eyes; he saw the amber liquid dripping off the nose she'd had modeled after Michelle Pfeiffer's; he watched her gasp in horror as the dress she'd probably paid at least three grand for was ruined. But he couldn't afford the satisfaction. He couldn't afford it as a kid, and he couldn't afford it now.

Inhaling deeply, Herb gripped his glass harder still, until he felt its sharply etched design bite deeply into his fingertips. The veins in his temples throbbed with frustration, but he didn't give in to it. "I'll put the ten thousand back in the bank as soon as the galleries' credit card payments are in for this month," he lied, keeping his voice calm and even. "Week after next, at the latest." There wouldn't really be anywhere near enough coming in from VISA and MasterCard to bail him out of this, but by then, Herb hoped, the first few bets he planned to place on the baseball playoffs would have paid off and he'd be flush again. He felt positive he had that meet pegged right, that his luck was about to turn around and he'd make a goddamned fortune. Kozlowski couldn't stop him. If his usual bookie would no longer take Herb's bets, he knew a few others who would.

"I'll believe that when I see my money," Jane said with a sigh. "I tell you, Herb, much as I hate to admit it, I'm beginning to think my father was right about you."

At the mention of the man who still managed to control so much of his life, even from the grave, Herb could no longer contain his anger. "Fuck your father and the horse he rode in on. The man was a goddamned liquor importer—not a rocket scientist. Or a marriage expert. And he sure as hell didn't walk on water."

"Fuck *you*, Herb! You never seem to mind spending Daddy's money, do you?" Jane's green eyes were cold as she turned on her heel and strutted toward the door in her strappy high-heeled shoes. "We're going to be late. Come on. We'll talk this out later."

She examined her makeup in the mirror above the small marble table by the front door, checking to see that her mascara was still intact and wiping at an invisible defect in her coral lipstick before she was completely satisfied. "I tell you," Jane said, grabbing the velvet-lined stole that matched her dress and tossing it around her shoulders, "if I wasn't introducing Dr. Perlmutter tonight, I'd say the hell with it and stay home. Thanks to you, my evening's ruined."

Herb downed the rest of his Scotch and set down his glass on the marble table. As he followed Jane out the front door, the keys to her dark green Jaguar in his hand, he couldn't help resenting the fact that she'd pledged five grand to this fancy shindig she was dragging him to. For her precious charity, the sky was the limit with her— "Daddy always told me that fortunate folks should give something back to society," she'd say in her self-righteous way.

Spending all her time on this crippled kids thing was all right, Herb supposed. Even tossing a few bucks their way wasn't too bad. She could afford it. But what about him? Hell, these could be the best years of his life if he wasn't caught in this goddamned vice, if only Jane would give him the benefit of the doubt once in a while. He couldn't see why she begrudged her own husband a measly ten grand he swore he needed for his shops. He thought his explanation about the missing money was a perfectly reasonable one. But no, she'd rather stick with her stupid notion that he had another woman stashed somewhere and keep him poverty-stricken.

Another woman! What a fool Jane was, Herb thought. Sex couldn't begin to compare with the rush he got whenever the jock or the team he'd bet on won, whenever his superior strategy paid off, whenever he beat the odds. It was the same kind of rush he used to feel back in the days when he was winning school swim meets, when he was a genuine sports hero himself and not just the housekeeper's back-street kid.

Still, whether Jane was deluded or not, Herb could see that getting his hands on her money was going to become more and more difficult. And he could also see Kozlowski and his enforcers rapidly closing in on him from the other direction.

As husband and wife reached the waiting Jaguar, Herb

spotted Louise Justman standing at her window, watching them as usual. "I knew Old Lady Justman would overhear us, the way you were yelling," he said to Jane.

Jane turned toward the house next door, her long copper hair swirling lightly around her face and shoulders. She spotted the woman peering out the window, met her squinty old eyes directly, and, unsmiling, gave a brief salute. With a quick shake of her head, Louise Justman took two quick steps backward and disappeared from view.

As he held the Jaguar's door open and waited while Jane carefully arranged her dress in the passenger seat so that it wouldn't wrinkle, Herb pictured his strong hands reaching for his wife's pretty neck. He saw them clench tighter and tighter until Jane's face turned blue and she no longer breathed—until she no longer had the power to deny him anything.

But once again, Herb Carmody controlled himself. A competitive swimmer knows he must wait for the starter's pistol before hitting the water, or he'll be disqualified, and a good gambler knows he has to keep a poker face. Herb had been a contestant in both of those worlds, and he'd learned the rules well.

But, as he climbed behind the wheel, he also knew that the turmoil in this marriage he'd entered for money was about to boil over. He was going to have to do something about Jane if he wanted to save himself.

Soon.

2

"Ellen!" Lightning cracked across the night sky. "Ellen!" The frantic voice was surprisingly strong. "Ellen! Come here, right now!"

Ellen Merchant set her book on the lamp table, pushed herself out of her rocking chair, and smoothed the skirt of her white cotton uniform before heading for the den, which nowadays served as a main floor bedroom. "I'm coming, Mrs. Edmonds," she called. From the note of panic she heard in Gladys Edmonds's voice, Ellen knew the old woman was having another bad night. Rainy weather always set Gladys on edge, particularly when thunder and lightning shook the rafters of her old three-story house. It had been raining in most of Minnesota all week and, by now, everyone's nerves were becoming frayed.

"Here I am, Mrs. Edmonds," Ellen said as she entered the room. "What can I do for you?" She tried her best to keep a friendly, reassuring smile on her face. Better Home Care, the St. Paul-based nursing service she worked for, stressed friendliness as an important part of the home-based assistance it provided to people like Gladys Edmonds, and Ellen was a conscientious employee.

"My sheets are all wrinkled up. And I need a drink of water." The terror the old woman's voice had held a moment ago began to turn into a whine now that the night nurse had arrived at her bedside.

Ellen suspected that what Gladys really wanted was some company. "I'll fix that," she said cheerfully. She quickly straightened the yellow flowered sheets on the mahogany four-poster and pulled up the lightweight blanket so that it covered Gladys's bony chest. "There. How's that?"

"Better."

Ellen poured some water from the carafe she kept on the bedside table into a glass, and cradled her patient's head while she took a sip. Thunder shook the house once more. Ellen could feel Gladys's body tremble as the window rattled in its frame. "Noisy out there tonight, isn't it?" Ellen kept her voice calm, reassuring.

Gladys swallowed another sip of the water, then turned her lips away from the glass. "When I was a child," she said, "my mother used to tell me thunder was God stomping across heaven on his way to punish a bad angel." Her old gray eyes looked frightened as she relived the memory. "She told me rain was the angels crying."

"Sounds pretty terrifying." Ellen's mind flashed onto an image of a girlish Gladys Edmonds, eighty or eighty-five years ago. She could see her cowering in her bed on rainy nights like this, terrified by the sounds of God's terrible wrath. Any child would be frightened under the circumstances. If the God she'd been taught to fear could become that angry with his angels—who were supposed to be intrinsically good—what horrible punishment might he have in store for a naughty little child? "I'll bet you were scared half to death when it rained like this," Ellen said, returning the water glass to the bedside table.

Gladys slid her withered hand across the bed covers toward the nurse.

Ellen covered it with her own lightly freckled hand and gave it a gentle squeeze. "Everything's going to be all right, Mrs. Edmonds," she said. "It's only a little thunder. And I'm right here with you."

The old woman's eyes grew moist. "I did it, too. Worse."

"What?"

"I did—I did the same thing to my own daughter, Sylvie."

"You did what, Mrs. Edmonds?"

"Told her that horrible story about God and the thunder. I—I told her if she wasn't a real good girl, God would come and take her away. I told her thunder was God's footsteps coming after her, 'cause she'd been such a bad girl."

Ellen tried to keep her voice nonjudgmental. "I guess all families pass down stories of one kind or another." Her own hadn't had much to pass on about God's wrath, or anything about God, for that matter. But there were plenty of other things to terrify Ellen and her older sister Claire while they were growing up. Ellen renewed a silent vow that, if she ever had children of her own, she'd stop and think before she said things that might frighten them unnecessarily, or burden them with unwarranted guilt. That she would keep herself from lashing out at them in anger—either with her tongue or with her fists.

The old woman's thin lips worked silently for a moment before she spoke again. "Sylvie had hair like yours when she was little."

Ellen twisted one of her ginger-colored curls around a finger. "Your daughter was a redhead?"

"I could always spot her in a crowd, her hair was so bright." Her eyelids fluttered closed for an instant, then opened again. "She was a pretty girl, like you." Ellen smiled. "I'm real sorry I told her that," Gladys said.

"About the thunder?"

Gladys nodded almost imperceptibly. "My poor little Sylvie was always scared of storms after that. I—I'm so sorry. Really I—"

"I'm sure Sylvie knew you didn't really mean to scare her." Ellen patted the old woman's hand. "Later, after she grew up, anyway."

"But I did," Gladys said as a tear escaped her eyelid and ran a crooked path down her wrinkled cheek. "That's what's so awful. I did mean to scare her. I wanted her to be a good girl and not give me any trouble and I—I guess I wanted her be to scared the way I was, too. I don't know why . . . Maybe I was just a bad mother."

Ellen shivered, although like most of the houses she'd worked in since she'd switched to private duty nursing, this one was overheated. Like now, her job often made her an unwilling witness to old people's confessions. As they crawled slowly toward death, the stories of their youthful exploits—their own personal Good Old Days—began to peter out and a desire to make amends for transgressions, both real and imagined, took over. Ellen wondered whether that was because they feared going to hell if they hadn't set things right before they died. Or simply because they genuinely regretted things they'd said or done.

Over the past few months, Ellen had heard more of her elderly patients' secrets than she could ever want to know—about how one had stolen two thousand dollars from his employer and was never caught, about another's history of extramarital affairs, about a third's giving up her infant twin sons for adoption when she was an unmarried teenager. Each story wrenched her heart as she did her best to reassure her charges. Still, she was no priest; she couldn't give anybody absolution. She was merely a sympathetic twenty-five-year-old nurse working private duty. A nurse who had plenty of her own personal demons to battle.

Gladys Edmonds was eighty-nine and her heart was nearly worn out. Ellen knew the old woman spent most of her time nowadays lying in this bed, dwelling on all the things she'd done that had hurt the people she loved. And, in eighty-nine years, she'd had plenty of time to collect a long, long list.

25

"We all do things we're sorry for afterward," Ellen said. "I'm sure Sylvie forgave you." Gladys had told Ellen that her daughter Sylvie had been dead for the past five years. She'd died of pancreatic cancer three days before her fifty-sixth birthday.

"I wish I knew for—" Gladys's voice became a whisper, then ceased altogether. Ellen held the withered hand for a few more minutes, until she was certain the old woman was once again asleep. She took her patient's pulse, made a note on the medical chart, and crept quietly out of the room.

Back in the kitchen, Ellen poured herself a cup of coffee and picked up her book, which had arrived in yesterday's mail. It was only a catalog, really, but it provided ample fuel for her fantasy life. Like Gladys Edmonds, Ellen needed something to occupy her mind during the long nights in this old house, during the lonely hours she spent waiting for the morning nurse to arrive and relieve her from duty.

Ellen didn't spend her time making mental lists of the sins she'd committed; there weren't really all that many, so far. Sometimes, though, listening to people like Gladys Edmonds brought back painful memories of her own early life—like the many times she'd hidden in the bedroom closet, her small hands clasped over her ears, as she tried to blot out the sounds of Mama beating Claire. Had Mama been sorry at the end? Probably not, Ellen decided. Mama probably had been too drunk to realize the harm she'd done her daughters. She'd died in an alcoholic haze, when Ellen was seven and Claire thirteen.

But Ellen didn't want to think about all that tonight. That was history, and she preferred to dream about the future, about all the places she wanted to see, the many exotic things she wanted to experience during her own remaining years. About escape.

By the time she was Mrs. Edmonds's age, Ellen Merchant planned to have lived a full life, to have seen the corners of the world, to have tasted new foods and new adventures. Unlike most of her patients, even most of her friends, Ellen had no intention of limiting her horizons to the Midwest. She wanted to see the French wine country, Venice's canals, New Zealand's fjords, every place that existed. If she could buy a ticket to the moon, Ellen would go there as well. Who knows, she thought, before her lifetime was over, a sightseeing trip to the moon might actually be a possibility. If it was, she would be first in line to buy a ticket.

Right now, there were only two things holding Ellen back from living the life of adventure she so craved—time and money. She'd already taken a big step toward remedying the first. Four months ago, she'd resigned her staff nursing job at Midway Hospital and signed on with Better Home Care, which allowed her to work as much or as little as she chose.

The disadvantage to private duty nursing was that she was stuck with the night shift and she found herself much more socially isolated than when she worked in the hospital. But the advantage was that she could call Better Home Care tomorrow and say she was going out of town for two weeks and she wouldn't endanger her job. She simply wouldn't collect a paycheck for hours she hadn't worked.

Solving the second problem was requiring a bit more effort. Ellen's monthly expenditures were not high and she had learned to be a thrifty young woman, but nursing was definitely not a high-paid profession. She had to budget her paycheck carefully to save anything at all.

Ellen lived in the small house she and Claire had inherited from their grandmother some eight years ago. Now Ellen paid the property taxes and sent Claire, who lived in Los Angeles, three hundred dollars a month in exchange for her sole use of the house. After making her car payment, paying her other bills, and budgeting every dollar she spent, Ellen was able to put aside three or four hundred dollars every month—provided that she worked a full schedule and didn't run into any emergency expenditures. Still, saving at that rate wasn't going to buy her many trips to Paris or Tokyo. Not if she had to stay in hotels and eat in restaurants once she got there, anyway.

Ellen hoped that the catalog she held in her hand would help make her dream of world travel a whole lot more feasible. Six months ago, at Claire's suggestion, she had joined the vacation home swapping club that printed catalogs like this one twice a year.

"I'm dying to exchange my apartment and take a nice vacation myself, Ellie," Claire had told her, "but my landlord lives in my building and he's a real stickler about the lease. No long-term guests, no parties, no smoking, no pets . . . no flexibility. I'm probably lucky Miser Morris lets me breathe the air around here. With rent control, he'd like nothing better than to get me out of here so he could charge somebody new higher rent. No way would he go for my letting strangers use my apartment when I wasn't there." Claire's voice grew wistful. "You don't know how lucky you are, having a whole house all to yourself."

Married friends of Claire's in Los Angeles had taken house exchange vacations in coastal Maine, Sweden and Holland over the past three years and had loved all of them. Best of all, except for the price of their airline tickets, their holidays had cost them little more than staying home would have. Claire good-naturedly admitted she was so envious of them she could hardly stand it.

At first, Ellen had shrugged off the idea of joining Claire's friends' club. As a nurse, she couldn't help feeling a little queasy about sleeping in some strangers' bed, bathing in their bathtub, and cooking in their kitchen. Not to mention those strangers staying in Ellen's own little house, using her bath towels, her bed sheets, her bedroom closet, her dishes and flatware. Not everybody was as neat and clean as she was.

Ellen's next-door neighbor, Vivian Henderson, added another concern. "Aren't you afraid strangers will steal your things?" she'd asked when Ellen mentioned Claire's suggestion to her. But Vivian had a tendency to zero in on the downside of anything; Ellen sometimes joked that, given half a second, Vivian could find fifteen negative aspects to winning the lottery.

Ellen had thought long and hard about Vivian's point, but eventually dismissed it. "Why would house exchangers be any more likely to steal from me than I am to steal from them?" she asked. "I'll be in their home using their things, too. Seems to me we'd all be in the same pickle."

In the end, the possibility that she might be able to take relatively cheap vacations to the exotic places she'd dreamed about seeing had overcome Ellen's reservations. So what if she had to do a little extra housecleaning, she told herself. That wasn't the end of the world.

So Ellen had sent in her ninety dollars and joined the club. Yesterday she'd received the second of the organization's two semi-annual catalogs; it was the first time her ad for her home was included.

Like many club members, Ellen had sent in two photographs with her written listing—one of her house, taken in the summertime when the trees along the boulevard and the marigolds in front of the house were in full bloom, and another of herself. Ellen's photo was the one she'd had taken for her nursing school graduation four years ago. She hoped that a picture of herself in her white uniform and peaked cap would inspire people to believe she was both trustworthy and clean. After all, who would object to having a nurse stay in their home? Added pluses were the facts that she had no children or pets and she didn't smoke. She hardly ever drank alcohol, either—she was too afraid of following in her drunken mother's footsteps. Ellen was the perfect house exchanger.

As rain pelted the kitchen window, the young nurse ran her finger lightly over her catalog entry. She was pleased with the way the words she'd written about herself and her house looked in print and excited about the prospect of receiving letters from other club members who wanted to come to Minnesota for a visit. She'd neglected to mention her region's often severe weather in her ad, rationalizing that spring and fall in the Twin Cities were often quite lovely.

Still, she knew she had a hard sell on her hands. When she joined the club, Ellen had written more than two dozen letters to members whose listings in an earlier catalog had intrigued her. But nobody had wanted to vacation in Minnesota. She was learning one of the cardinal rules of home exchanging—people with houses in exotic vacation locales generally wanted to trade them for equally desirable spots. Paris for London. Los Angeles for New York City. Carmel for Hawaii. Colorado's ski country for Palm Beach. While Minnesota was a good, safe place to live and raise children, it wasn't exactly most folks' idea of a dream travel destination. Although Ellen herself was a highly desirable exchange prospect, her house was not.

But she wasn't about to give up. As her patient snored peacefully in her bed down the hall and the storm outside gradually blew itself out, Ellen examined page after page, searching for anybody who expressed a desire to vacation in her hometown. She found only two—a librarian in Duluth who wanted to come to the Twin Cities for a convention and a farmer in northern Iowa who wanted to try a week of city life next winter, when his fields would be idle and he could get away. Neither held much appeal for her, so she turned to those who were more flexible about their stated desires, the ones whose listings—like her own—said they would consider exchanging homes anytime, anywhere.

By the time the storm had ended and the first daylight crept through the kitchen windows, Ellen had marked thirty-two catalog entries for homes in places as far flung as Geneva, Mexico City, Aspen, and Honolulu. This afternoon, after she'd had a few hours of sleep, she would begin writing to all of them.

With a bit of luck and timing, Ellen Merchant assured herself as she set out her patient's morning medications, she would soon escape to that faraway world she'd been dreaming about.

3

Herb kept staring at the big screen long after the game was over, straight through all the beer commercials and into the news promo, as though concentrating hard enough might somehow change the final score. Who knew the Giants would cinch the Western Division and then fade to black on their own turf, losing three of their five games over the weekend?

"How 'bout them Giants?" A bony hand pounded Herb's back, startling him out of his stupor. He turned to see Sid Balzarian, another of the sports bar's regulars, standing next to him, wearing tight jeans, cowboy boots, and a plaid shirt with a string tie. The mug of brew in Sid's other hand was dripping suds onto the sawdust-covered floor. The two men had spent countless hours together here at Jocks, watching games they'd both bet on.

Herb grimaced. "Sonofabitch pitcher just cost me five grand," he said. He'd figured on doubling the five thousand he bet on the Giants and using his take to hold off Kozlowski for a little while longer. But now—

Sid whistled. "You had five big ones on the Giants today?" Herb nodded, despondent. "Hell, thought I was a big spender with my pissy two hundred on Seattle," Sid said.

"Least you picked the right team." Herb said. "Christ, Sid, my luck's turned to complete shit. Last week the A's went down against Anaheim and today the Giants tank. Between the two of them, I kissed off ten grand. Hell, I feel like I'm bombing out of the Olympic trials all over again."

Sid slid into the chair opposite Herb's and leaned across the table. "Used to be a swimmer, right?"

"Distance swimmer. Fifteen-hundred-meter freestyle. Shit! I came this close, Sid—" Herb held his index finger an inch away from his thumb to illustrate. "—this close to making the nineteen-eighty-four U.S. Olympic team and then who knows. Could've had endorsements, TV commercials, my own swimwear, maybe even home swimming pools. Big bucks. But that Michigan State kid aced me out in the final heat by a lousy tenth of a second. A tenth of a second and I'm a has-been! Screwed me out of the whole damn prize and—"

"Yeah, yeah, you told me a hundred times. Tough break. But, hey, win a few, lose a few."

Herb glared resentfully at Balzarian's self-satisfied grin. What did this short, skinny guy with the leathery face and the graying Elvis Presley haircut really know about competition? What did this small time gambler know about pushing it to the limit, about putting yourself on the line, about blasting the competition right out of the water? Hell, Sid thought a two-hundred-dollar wager was a big fucking deal. "If it hadn't been for that Mich—"

"Dirty shame, but hey, lighten up. I'm celebratin' here. Next round's on me. Pick your poison."

Did the man ever say anything that wasn't a cliche? Herb wondered. He looked down at his half-empty mug. He'd been nursing his third draft beer for the past hour and what was left was now warm and flat. He didn't really come to Jocks to drink; he came to see the games on big screen TV and to share a sense of camaraderie with the other sports fans cheering on their chosen teams. He slid his mug to the other side of the table. He knew he should go back to Waves. His art gallery was just around the corner on Jefferson Street, not far from San Francisco's Pier 39. He should see whether Ginny and Sue had locked the place up properly at closing time, whether they'd managed to sell anything at all this afternoon. But right now he really didn't give a damn. All Herb wanted to do was sink into a deep dark hole somewhere, someplace where Kozlowski and his goons would never find him. Hide deep in the water, like one of those sleek sharks in the paintings he sold at Waves. "Scotch," Herb said after a moment's hesitation, "a double." Something stronger than beer might take the edge off his blue funk, he thought. The price was right and he was certainly in no rush to get home. Going home to Jane in the mood he was in would only make everything worse.

Sid waved for the bartender, then ordered a double Cutty Sark for Herb and a beer for himself. When their drinks had arrived, Sid raised his mug in a toast. "To better luck next time." Sid Balzarian had never been known for his original speech pattern, but he had a sharp eye for an opportunity and Herb Carmody was wearing a look of desperation that was familiar to him. That kind of look often told Sid that a guy was ripe for a con, and he'd been sizing up Herb Carmody for months now.

Herb gulped his Scotch. It wasn't as smooth as the stuff he drank at home—Jane always had the Tiburon liquor store deliver Glenlivet—but it would have to do. By the time he drained his glass, he was beginning to feel a bit mellower and his worry about Kozlowski and his debt collectors was beginning to dim.

"Lucky for you, you can afford to drop five K on a Sunday's entertainment," Sid suggested, signaling the bartender to bring Herb another double. "Loss like that'd set me back for months."

"Dream on." Herb's shoulders slumped lower as he leaned forward in his chair, his elbows on the table. He started on the fresh Scotch as soon as the bartender set it down in front of him.

Sid laughed. He'd known Herb Carmody for nearly two years and he'd never seen him watch a game he didn't have a bet riding on. "Who're you kiddin'? You're not hurtin'. I was married to an heiress, I guess five grand'd be pocket change to me, too."

Herb sucked down his second drink. "Married to a fortune don't mean you got a fortune, Sid. Remember that. That's lesson number one. Lesson number two—" He took another gulp of scotch. By the time it hit his stomach, he couldn't remember lesson number two. "Lesson number—" His voice trailed off.

Sid ordered Herb another Scotch. His own beer had barely been touched. "You tryin' to tell me that wife of yours ain't sharin' the wealth?"

Herb's face began to go slack now and he had to think slowly and carefully to make his words come out right. He'd never been a good drinker and the Scotch was hitting him quick and hard on his empty stomach. Lunch had been three or four stale tortilla chips with some foul-smelling salsa. "Lemme tell you somethin', pal," he said, finally. "Lady Jane's the stingy—stingiest bitch ever born. Writes these big checks for all this charity crap and don't give me shit."

"You're puttin' me on, Herb. Somebody's gotta be stakin' you, you bet five grand on a baseball game ain't even the World Series. Hell, I've seen that shop of yours, your art gallery. Not exactly a gold mine, am I right?" Waves had some nice stuff in it, Sid thought, if you were into paintings of old ships and brass sea otters and stuff like that, but any fool could see it would never support the kind of betting—and losing—that Herb Carmody had been doing lately. His money had to be coming from somewhere—probably his wife—and Sid intended to cash in himself, if possible. He was tired of running his usual scams on San Francisco's gullible elderly, the kind that netted him a few hundred bucks here and there. If he could make one really big score, he'd retire in a second. He bought Herb another drink and continued trying to pick the man's brain, but he learned little.

Half an hour later, Herb was finishing his fourth double Scotch. The glass made a hollow bang as he set it down on the tabletop too hard. His vision was blurry now and the din of the television set and the other drinkers became less and less distinct for him.

"Come on, Herb, give." Sid was quickly losing patience.

"What?"

"Where're you gettin' all that dough?"

"Dough? Ain't gettin', thas problem. Koz—Kozlowski's gonna have my ass, my luck don' change real quick."

"Whadya mean?"

"Shit, man, gave 'im twenty-five big ones last week. Gotta come up wi' 'nother twenty-five every week, plus interest. Gotta make a killing, get out from under."

"Jesus. You owe Kozlowski twenty-five K a week?" Sid's eyes widened.

Herb nodded woozily.

"That's dangerous, man, to run up a bill like that with Kozlowski. You don't wanna be pissin' off a guy like that."

"No shit."

"Can't you ask your old lady to advance you some cash? I mean, she ain't gonna want Kozlowski takin' it out of your hide, right?"

"You—you don' know 'er. She—" Herb's eyes slowly closed and his shoulders drooped forward until his head hit the table with a light thud. The conversation was over.

Sid sighed and rolled his eyes. The man obviously couldn't hold his liquor. He'd wanted Herb loosened up, sure, but he wasn't going to get any useful information out of Sleeping Beauty here, not until he sobered up some, anyway. Waste of half a bottle of Scotch. He pushed away his beer mug and ordered two cups of strong black coffee. When it arrived, he gripped Herb by his mop of dark blond hair, lifted the drunken man's head off the plastic-topped table, and shoved a coffee cup under his nose.

"Wake up, Herb," Sid ordered as the steam from the coffee invaded Herb's nostrils. The drunken man flinched and his sagging eyelids flitted open again. "Drink up, pal," Sid told him.

Herb drank with a harsh slurping sound. "Hot!" he wheezed, spitting half of the steaming liquid back into the cup and pushing it away. He teetered in his seat for a moment, but remained generally upright.

"Just sit there a minute, let the coffee cool," Sid said. "I'll drive you home." Maybe his investment in the Scotch wouldn't be a total loss after all. Driving Herb Carmody home would give Sid a chance to see where the man lived, maybe even get a look at the heiress. There had to be some angle he could work here.

"Can't," Herb said. "Gotta get my car home. Need it tomorrow."

"So I'll drive your car. I see Barry O'Farrell sittin' over there." He gave a wave to a paunchy, balding ex-bouncer sitting alone at a table across the room, nursing a draft beer. "Barry's a good guy and he's got wheels. He won't mind followin' us over the bridge and givin' me a ride back to the city."

"Dunno, Sid—"

"Look, buddy, you try to drive in your condition, you're gonna end up in jail or the bay, trust me."

Herb nodded sleepily. At some primitive level concerned

with self-preservation, he knew it would be suicide for him to try driving across the Golden Gate Bridge to Tiburon any-time soon. He probably should go back to the gallery, sleep it off there. But then Jane would be pissed as hell at him . . . again. There was something, some shindig they were sched-uled to go to tonight. If only he could remember what it was. "Charity thing," he said out loud.

"What'd you say?"

"Jane. Gotta go to some charity thing with her tonight. 'S where all her money goes. Time, too. Dresses up in a fuckin' clown suit for a bunch o' kids ain't even hers."

"You tellin' me your wife writes big checks for charity and she won't buy your butt outta trouble with Kozlowski?"

"Don't know 'bout Kozlowski. Jane finds out 'bout Kozlowski, I'm out on my ass." Herb sipped at his coffee. It was cooler now. He took a long drink. Damn, he'd really screwed up this time. On Friday, he'd taken some of Jane's jewelry—the emerald-and-pearl earrings and necklace she'd worn to last week's fundraising dinner—out of the safe de-posit box at the bank and pawned it to make the rest of last week's payment to Kozlowski. But even after he made the week's payment the bookie'd demanded, he wouldn't let Herb place a bet on today's game. He'd had to go to Wo Fat in Chinatown for that action, and that meant paying cash up front, the full five thousand. If the fucking Giants had only won the way they were supposed to, Herb thought, he'd have had an extra five grand in his hand right now, enough to place a few more bets. By the end of the week, with a little luck, he'd have been able to get Jane's jewelry back out of hock be-fore she knew it was gone and to make another payment on his tab with Kozlowski.

Sid leaned back in his chair and thought for a moment. If what Herb was telling him was fact, it was obvious that the gambler himself wasn't the one to con here. You wanted to get money out of Herbert Carmody, you were gonna have to get in line behind Kozlowski, not a comfortable position to be in. The wife, on the other hand, was loaded. The challenge here was to get her to part with her money. Herb said she gave money to charity. That was something. Maybe there was some charity angle Sid could work here. And like he'd always said, charity begins at home.

"I don't get it, Herb," Sid said. "California's a community property state, right? How come you can't just take some of your wife's money and use it to pay off Kozlowski?"

"Inherited."

"Huh?"

"Inherited money ain't community property."

"That right?"

Herb drained the cup and felt his stomach lurch. "Gotta take a leak." He got slowly to his feet and staggered toward the men's room, where he quickly vomited up most of what he'd drunk. In the end, as he knelt on the floor, his head hanging over the stinking toilet bowl and his eyes stinging, the only thing that remained in his stomach was raw fear.

While Herb was in the men's room, Sid sauntered across the bar and approached Barry O'Farrell. For a ten-spot and half a tank of gas, Barry was happy to follow the two men across the bridge to Tiburon, then chauffeur Sid back to the city.

In the meantime, Sid's mental wheels would be turning. He knew there had to be an angle he could play here. It was simply a matter of finding it and playing it out.

4

Her house key clutched in her hand, Claire Merchant climbed the concrete stairs leading to her second floor Santa Monica apartment. Her steps were slow and heavy after her long day's efforts. Today, she'd done four interviews for the article on battered women she was writing for *Glamour*, driving from her Santa Monica apartment north to a battered women's shelter in Reseda, then sixty miles south to Long Beach and finally back home again. After hearing so much about boyfriends and husbands who'd beaten, burned, stabbed, even murdered their wives and girlfriends, Claire couldn't help feeling depressed as well as exhausted.

Certainly her article would help to shed light on a terrifying aspect of modern sexual relationships, Claire told herself. Her written words would warn *Glamour*'s readers about the signs of potential abuse to watch for in their romances. Undoubtedly, she was performing a valuable service for other women. Still, Claire knew she was going to have to come up with some more cheerful topics to write about—and soon—if she wanted to retain her own emotional equilibrium.

Last month she'd done a piece on sexual harassment in the movie business for *Working Woman*—another downer—and a few weeks before that she'd written a profile of two counselors at Santa Monica Hospital's Rape Crisis Center for the *Los Angeles Times*. Those articles followed the three-thousand-word feature she'd written about a safe house for mothers and their sexually abused children. She'd sold that one to *Ladies' Home Journal*.

Lately, although Claire hadn't consciously realized she'd

been heading in that direction, her writing career was turning into an exploration of the many ways in which women and children become victims of abuse. Had she been trying to convince herself that other people's lives were far more screwed up than her own? Or simply that there was life after abuse?

Relationships didn't have to include violence and heartache, of course. Claire firmly believed that. But with her recent dreams replaying her nasty childhood for her, and the court hearing on her divorce scheduled for next month, she'd been feeling pretty victimized herself lately. Interviewing and writing about women who were far worse off served as a kind of psychotherapy for her—something she needed but couldn't possibly afford on her sporadic freelance earnings. At thirty-one and after six years of marriage, Claire Merchant was completely on her own financially, with her divorce attorney's bill due shortly.

Claire unlocked the door and headed through her nearly empty living room to her office in the apartment's back bedroom. Her rent-controlled place was tiny, and it seemed even more depressing now that it was half empty of furnishings. She'd let her husband Charlie take most of the living room and dining room furniture to his new place when he moved out, salvaging only an overstuffed blue chair, an end table and lamp, and the bedroom things in addition to her office furniture and computer equipment.

Anything to keep the peace, she'd thought at the time. Anything to ease her guilt over rejecting her husband, over being the one who'd decided to call it quits. Now that she had only the easy chair, plus an old card table and four folding chairs to furnish her main living area, however, Claire wasn't so sure her decision had been a good one. It would be a long, long time before she could afford new furniture.

As she headed into her office, Claire's eye fell on the phone machine. The yellow light was blinking and the electronic display told her she had two messages. Tossing her notebook, tape recorder, and purse on the desk, she tucked a strand of her long, golden brown hair behind an ear, picked up a pencil, and punched the replay button.

"Hi, Claire, sorry I missed you." Claire recognized her sister Ellen's voice on the tape and, for the first time in several hours, a smile began to play across her suntanned face. "Listen, I'm writing a bunch of letters for this house exchange thing you got me into and I had another one of my famously brilliant thoughts," Ellen said. "If I score big on this, how about you coming with me? London, Honolulu, New York, Switzerland, whatever's the best I can arrange. Could be fun, you and me doing something together again, right? Without crappy old Charlie to ruin things. Listen, I'm working tonight, but I'll try you again in the morning, before I go to bed." Ellen's voice took on a wheedling tone that was familiar to her older sister. "And don't just say you can't get away, Claire. At least *think* about coming with me, okay? You need a vacation as much as I do, so this time, just do it. 'Bye."

Ellen was right, Claire had to admit. She did need a vacation. There was nothing she'd love better than to fly away to some exotic place, to escape. Right now.

Claire also recognized the voice on her second phone message. The momentary good mood her sister's call had sparked quickly vanished as she heard her soon-to-be ex-husband Charlie's angry words.

"I brought back your precious books and your so-called novel," he said, the last word ripe with sarcasm. "So maybe now you can get off my fuckin' back." Claire winced as a sharp cracking sound told her Charlie had slammed down the receiver, ending his call.

This kind of message was nothing new from Charlie McVee. Her husband's rage had permeated all of their conversations over the past six months, ever since the day Claire told him the marriage wasn't working for her anymore, that she could no longer live with his drinking and his explosive temper. Ever since she'd asked him to move out of the apartment. That Charlie would be the one to move out was the only condition about which Claire hadn't compromised. Without this rent-controlled place to live in, she would have a hard time staying in the Los Angeles area. Her husband, on the other hand, had a management job with a restaurant chain that paid him a good salary and full benefits. He could afford to pay a whole lot more rent.

Claire looked around her, but saw none of her books and papers that Charlie had taken with him when he'd moved out. There was no stack on her desktop or box on the floor. She quickly checked the living room and the kitchen. Nothing.

"You playing one of your stupid games with me again, Charlie?" Claire asked out loud. The man's anger was contagious. She simply couldn't deal with him anymore without ending up feeling infuriated. She hadn't felt this much impotent rage since she was an adolescent, fending off one of her mother's drunken rampages. As then, now she wasn't sure she knew the best way to defend herself against the attack of an irrationally angry person.

Claire headed for the bedroom, looking in the closet and under the bed, but the delivery Charlie claimed he'd made wasn't there, either. What else was new, she thought. Charlie'd always been unreliable, and he lied whenever it suited his purpose. After he moved out, he claimed he'd taken her things with him inadvertently, that she must have put them in his bookcase in the living room by mistake. Nobody could blame him for packing them up. The whole thing

43

was obviously her fault for mixing her things in with his.

But Claire knew she hadn't done that. She'd never kept her books and papers anywhere but in her own office. The truth was, when he moved out, Charlie had simply stolen her entire shelf of reference books—a dictionary, a thesaurus, *The Elements of Style*, three or four books of famous quotes and the like—as well as the typed copy of the novel she'd worked on intermittently for years.

He'd done it purely for spite, of course; Claire knew that. She'd had to have her attorney write Charlie three threatening letters before he finally agreed to bring her things back. Now he claimed he'd actually done just that.

But where the hell were they?

"Damn you, Charlie," Claire said as she hung her suit jacket in the bedroom closet and stepped out of her skirt. After pulling on jeans and a T-shirt, she headed back through the kitchen to the tiny bathroom to freshen up before dinner. Her solitary meal would undoubtedly be her usual supermarket frozen entree and a salad, assuming the package of mixed greens she'd bought last week at the Santa Monica Farmer's Market was still salvageable.

As she pushed open the door to the white-tiled bathroom, Claire stopped short and the hairs on the back of her neck stood on end. Something wasn't right; she could feel it, and she could hear it. The shower curtain was closed and an intermittent dripping sound was coming from behind it. She was certain she'd left the curtain open after her shower this morning. Now the curtain—an opaque plastic sheet printed with a montage of famous newspaper headlines—was drawn tightly closed across the bathtub.

Claire stood rigid for a moment, all of her senses on full alert. "Charlie, are you in there?" she demanded. "Charlie?" She heard only an occasional drip-drip-drip, no human voice or sounds of breathing. Swallowing her fear, Claire reached over and yanked the shower curtain open.

As her mind took in the scene behind the plastic curtain, a harsh cry emerged from somewhere deep inside her. It was a mournful sound, not unlike the cries the women she'd interviewed today must have uttered when an angry lover caught them with a sharp blow across the face.

In the bathtub lay the entire manuscript of Claire's novel-in-progress, along with the reference books she'd used so often in her work.

Charlie had made his delivery, all right. He'd dumped all of Claire's belongings into the bathtub. Then he'd filled it with water.

Her eyes quickly filling with tears, Claire dropped to her knees and began to pull soggy sheets of paper from the tepid pool of water.

As her work shredded and dissolved in her fingers, she sobbed, "You goddamned son of a bitch!"

5

Herb sat at his desk in the back room of Waves II, the newer of his two art galleries, which was located on Tiburon's Main Street. He was nursing the worst hangover he'd had in years. His stomach was still queasy, but whether the excess Scotch he'd drunk yesterday was the only culprit was debatable. The fingers of fear reaching down into his intestines and squeezing hard certainly were contributing to his agony.

"I've got some aspirin in my purse, Herb. Want a couple?" Marlene LeBaron asked sympathetically. Marlene had been Herb's employee ever since the first Waves opened in San Francisco. Now she was frequently left in charge of Waves II whenever Herb was away from the shop. A tall, eminently reliable woman in her mid-forties, she had a strong tendency to mother her boss.

"Had two at lunch." Herb checked his watch. It was now nearly four o'clock. "Guess another couple won't kill me." He held out his palm as Marlene plopped two round white pills into it.

"Hard night?" she asked.

"You don't know the half of it." After Sid Balzarian drove him back to Tiburon, Herb had been in no shape to attend that benefit dinner with Jane. Staggering and stinking of booze and vomit, for once he couldn't really blame his wife for the cold shoulder she gave him. He couldn't remember why he'd drunk so much, either. Sure, he'd been distraught about the five grand he'd lost, but it wasn't like him to get drunk. At least not that drunk.

Today, Herb was worried half sick. Even as sloshed as he

was last night, he'd been able to recognize the danger signs—Jane was very close to giving up on him and their marriage. She wasn't going to tolerate many more of his screw-ups, any fool could see that. If he didn't do something soon to turn things around, Jane was going to feed him to the sharks.

Last night, she'd taken one look at his physical condition and lit into him, not even waiting to start her recriminations until Sid Balzarian and Barry O'Farrell had driven away from the house. That Mrs. Justman next door had heard the whole thing was a given. Then Jane put on her long silk coat and drove herself to another of her charity dinners, leaving Herb to clean himself up as best he could.

Jane had never gone to one of those evening events by herself before. She'd always needed her good-looking husband beside her, to prop her up if she had one of her old attacks of crippling shyness. The fact that she'd left him behind last night had Herb's stomach churning almost as much as his hangover did. Last night seemed too much like a dress rehearsal for the life his wife probably was planning to spend without him. It was all beginning to fit together—Jane's new nose, her new wardrobe, her newfound self-confidence, the satisfaction she seemed to be getting lately from her work on behalf of handicapped kids. Did she really still need her husband to feel complete, or was he becoming expendable?

Marlene brought Herb a coffee cup filled with water from the cooler. "Want to talk about it, Herb?"

He washed the aspirins down with a swallow of water. "Thanks, but no." There was no percentage in involving his employees in his personal troubles, Herb decided. He forced his thoughts back to the gallery. "That Phil Harrigan's seascapes?"

Marlene had been pulling nails out of a large wooden crate in the corner of the gallery's back room. "Nope, it's from

47

Charlotte Windsor. Today's UPS delivery isn't here yet. Phil's stuff will probably be in it. Or else tomorrow's." Marlene returned to her task and pulled out another nail, letting it drop to the rough wooden floorboards. "Don't know where we're going to put Harrigan's new paintings anyway."

Business was getting worse in both of the Waves galleries. The biggest part of the tourist season was already over for the year. There might be a surge in business just before Christmas, but otherwise Herb had to admit the outlook was dismal. As a result, stock like Phil Harrigan's realistic paintings of the rugged Northern California coastline was moving slowly, if at all.

"Figure we'll move out some of the historicals." Herb's reference was to a group of early twentieth century paintings of clipper ships that had been hanging in the front of the Tiburon shop all summer long, gathering more dust than sales. "Nobody seems to want them."

"Okay, but if Harrigan sends the full half dozen you asked for, we're still going to be overcrowded." Marlene removed the last of the nails and pried the cover off the crate. It fell to the floor with a bang that reverberated through Herb's aching head. He pressed his fingers hard against his temples in a futile attempt to get relief.

"Leave some of them back here, then," he mumbled. "Change them every week or ten days. Can't have the place looking cluttered." Herb knew that trying to display too much art in too small a space meant that nothing was shown off to its best advantage. As a result, the back room of Waves II often held more works of art than the showroom did.

Marlene pulled off the front panel of the crate, then attempted to slide the object inside it out onto the floor, but it was too heavy for her. "How about a hand over here?" she asked. "Don't want to damage this piece." Or her back, either, she thought.

Herb grunted agreement, moving slowly toward the spot where his employee was laboring, trying his best not to jar his aching head in the process.

"Here," Marlene said, "you pull on his head and I'll pull on his tail." The two pushed through a mound of Styrofoam packing pellets and, after a couple of aborted tries, slid a life-size pelican, regal in its pose, out of the depths of the packing crate.

"Christ, this thing weighs a ton," Herb complained as they moved the big bird away from its wooden packaging.

"Solid marble, except for that brass base. Like all of Charlotte's work." They turned the pelican around on the floor and Marlene quickly dusted off the last few Styrofoam particles sticking to its carved stone feathers.

Despite his aching head, Herb had to admire the stately gray-toned creature standing before him. He ran his hands slowly over the marble, feeling its perfectly smooth cool surface beneath his fingertips. "Incredible piece of work."

"Might be Charlotte's best so far. Although for my money, it's hard to top that harbor seal and pup she did for us last year."

It was because of moments like this that Herb Carmody had opened his art galleries in the first place—that flash of sheer pleasure he felt whenever he saw a wonderful new piece of art and realized it was his. Of course, many of the pieces displayed in Waves and Waves II didn't really belong to him; he offered them for sale on consignment, forwarding half the purchase price to the artists after they were sold. If he had to purchase his art outright, he'd never be able to stock his shops with quality artworks like Charlotte Windsor's remarkable marble and stone sculptures of marine creatures.

The truth was, the galleries were a substitute for what Herb really dreamed of having—his own private art collection, one that celebrated his lifelong affinity for the sea, for water. If he'd realized his dream of Olympic fame and built a financial empire upon it—or if his wife's money was his own—he would never have bothered with the two shops. He'd simply have bought the artworks he loved and filled his own home with them. On good days, he still believed he would have that kind of money someday.

He probably wouldn't live in Jane's Tiburon house, though, despite its incomparable view. More likely, he'd buy one of those huge old mansions in San Francisco's Pacific Heights district, the kind of place with rooms large enough to hold a full-size pelican sculpture like this one, along with half a dozen other beautiful and valuable pieces of art. Or, better yet, he'd have the kind of mansion that came with acres of grounds, like the Santa Barbara estate where he'd grown up. He'd always dreamed of owning a home like the last place he and his mother had lived when he was a kid. An estate like the one where, as a teenager, he'd shoveled out the stables of horses he was never allowed to ride, where he'd cleaned the pool in which he was never allowed to swim.

It was Jane, not Herb, who'd wanted to move far away from Santa Barbara, to San Francisco. Herb liked San Francisco well enough, but he'd have preferred staying nearer to their old haunts. He'd have preferred rubbing a few rich snobs' noses in his own newfound wealth. It was Jane's idea for them to start a whole new life, to go someplace where nobody knew about her painful girlhood, where people didn't look down on her because her money came from the liquor business. It was her idea that Herb should go into business for himself, become a success in his own right. Things hadn't worked out quite as she'd planned, however. After moving to

San Francisco, she remained self-conscious and shy, and she didn't socialize much. Things hadn't really started to change for her until a year ago, after her father died and she decided to see a plastic surgeon. Now that she'd become a pretty woman, Herb could tell that Jane was beginning to feel like that whole new person she wanted to be.

Marlene and Herb wrestled the pelican to the center of the gallery, where they hoisted it onto a short boxy pedestal for display. "Price is twelve-five, right?" Marlene asked as she headed back toward her desk in the back room to make out a discreetly small price card.

"Think so. Check the agreement letter," Herb replied. Beautiful as the pelican was, he knew it would probably take months to find a buyer willing to pay more than twelve grand for a stone, four-foot-high sculpture of a bird. Sometimes he thought he'd have been better off if he'd opened a poster shop or converted Waves to the kind of place that sold T-shirts to tourists. Still, if he gave up the galleries now, he'd end up with nothing. All the time and effort he'd put into his shops would be down the toilet.

"Talk to Ginny yet?" Marlene asked as she bent down to tape the hand-lettered price card to the pelican's pedestal.

"Ginny? About what?"

Marlene stood up again and flicked a shred of Styrofoam off her skirt. "My vacation next month."

Herb's face remained blank.

"Herb, I asked you about it a good six weeks ago, remember?" He nodded vaguely. "You said you'd have Ginny take over for me here. Nick and I are all set to go to Paris."

"Paris! You and Nick are going to Paris? Old Nick must have gotten himself a helluva nice raise." Herb knew that Marlene's salary and commission from Waves II wouldn't bankroll a trip like that; her husband Nick must have cashed in somewhere. Maybe he'd bet on the Yankees last night.

"Don't I wish. Nick and I both could use a good raise." Marlene stared pointedly at Herb, but he didn't look the least bit embarrassed by her hint. "We're doing a house exchange in Paris, that's all," she said. "It'll save us a good three thousand on hotel bills, not to mention we won't have to eat in restaurants all the time."

Herb moved through the curtain into the back room. His head still ached and he wasn't really paying much attention to Marlene's excited chatter. But Marlene seemed to interpret his occasional grunts and nods as interest in her vacation plans.

"We're going to do the usual tourist stuff like the Eiffel Tower and the Arc de Triomphe, of course, but what I really can't wait to see is the Louvre."

"Sure you'll still want to come back to work here after you've seen all the old masters?"

Humming "I Love Paris" to herself, Marlene opened her desk drawer and pulled out a catalog. "Listen, if the Louvre tries to hire me to manage its marine art collection," she said, "I'm out of here in a flash . . . but I don't think you're going to lose much sleep over that possibility." Grinning, she opened the book to a place she had marked and carried it over to Herb's desk. "See? Here's the house we're going to stay in." She plopped the book down in front of him and pointed to a small yellow brick building scrunched in amongst others like it.

In an effort to be polite, Herb focused on the spot Marlene indicated. "Looks okay, I guess."

"Okay? Okay? Geez, Herb, this place is on the Left Bank, right across the bridge from the Place de la Concorde. Right on top of everything we want to see. You know what a hotel in that neighborhood costs these days? In American dollars?"

Double or Nothing

Herb shook his head. It still throbbed. "I don't know, a hundred-fifty a night, maybe."

"Yeah, right. Not anytime in the past decade. Try three hundred, three-fifty. Lucky the only things Nick and I are going to have to pay for are our airline tickets and stuff like groceries and tickets to get into the museums."

"How about taxis?"

Marlene grinned. "No problem. We've even got a car to use in Paris. Comes with the house. And whenever it doesn't make sense to drive somewhere, we'll just take the Metro. At least that's still cheap."

Herb glanced down at the book Marlene had spread out on his desk. "What is this thing anyway?"

Marlene walked around the desk and leaned over her boss's shoulder. "Sort of a club. Costs ninety bucks a year for two books like these, including your listing. If you want to include a photo or two, they're ten dollars apiece." As she explained the house exchange concept in more detail than Herb thought he could ever want to know, she flipped through the catalog's pages, each of which included perhaps thirty listings. Highlights of each ad were written in English, followed by a number of additional details in code.

"What do all these hieroglyphics mean?" Herb asked, trying to show polite interest in his employee's passion.

"Each symbol stands for something. Like VW means your house has a view, EK means electric kitchen, like that. That way you can get a lot more information into your space and people who don't read English can just decipher the code in their own language."

Marlene went on to explain that she and her husband had done house exchanges twice before. The first time, they'd gone to Lake Tahoe in wintertime and the second was a trip to Washington, D.C. This was to be their first trip abroad in

53

their twenty-two years of marriage. "I'm getting all excited just telling you about it," she said.

Herb could see that Marlene's face was aglow with anticipation. A strong pang of envy coursed through him and he wished he were looking forward to a vacation trip like his employee's, a chance to get away from San Francisco with nothing more on his mind than having a good time, seeing someplace new. He lowered his gaze before Marlene could guess what he was thinking and began absent-mindedly paging through the catalog. "Your photo in here?" he asked.

Marlene blushed slightly. "No, Nick said we shouldn't risk scaring potential exchangers off." An embarrassed chuckle escaped from her lips. Marlene was not unattractive, but at forty-four, she tended toward plumpness, and at a full five feet eight inches tall, she was definitely a large woman. Her husband, Nick, was almost totally bald at fifty and his front teeth protruded. His lifelong self-consciousness about his teeth made him hold his hand over his mouth whenever he laughed or smiled. At best, the LeBarons were average looking. "Lots of folks do put their photos in, though," Marlene said.

"Most of these look pretty air-brushed to me," Herb said as he turned pages. "Not a wrinkle or a pimple in sight." Now he was into the section that listed homes in the United States. A handsome young doctor from Maine stared from one page, wearing a gray suit and crisp blue shirt. His blonde wife could have been a cover girl. On the next, Herb's gaze fell upon an earnest-looking gray-haired couple from Boston. The wife held an angora cat in her lap. He wondered idly how many house exchangers would want to welcome Tabby into their homes along with Grandma and Grandpa here.

As Herb turned more pages, a photo leapt out at him. In the center of the meagre Minnesota section, it was a picture of a smiling young woman in a nurse's uniform and cap. But it wasn't the nurse's pretty freckled face that caught Herb's attention. It was her hair. Escaping from under her cap was a cascade of curls, all of them a brilliant russet. At first glance the nurse looked disturbingly like his wife Jane with her new nose.

"If you're interested in joining, I'll copy the application form for you," Marlene suggested.

"Huh? Oh, no thanks." Herb realized he'd been transfixed on the young Minnesota woman's photograph. As he slapped the catalog shut and handed it back to Marlene, the seed of an idea began sprouting in his sodden mind. The last thing he wanted was for what he was thinking to show on his face. "This kind of thing's not for me," he said.

"Why not?"

Herb thought fast. He could tell the truth, of course, that as a kid he'd spent far too many years living in other people's houses to consider doing it again to be a vacation. Jane would never go for the idea, either. She wouldn't like letting some stranger into her house. But then, Jane could afford to stay in the best hotels anywhere in the world if she wanted to travel. Herb didn't want to bring Jane into this conversation, however. "The idea of somebody staying in my house," he said finally, "using my things, all that . . . Doesn't appeal to me, that's all."

Marlene shrugged her shoulders and carried the catalog to her desk. "Whatever," she said as she slid it into her top drawer. "Anyway, don't forget I'll be gone from the tenth to the twenty-seventh."

"I'll mark my calendar and talk to Ginny about ferrying over from the city for those days."

At six-thirty, after Waves II was locked up for the day and

Marlene had gone home, Herb opened her desk and removed the house exchange catalog. It took him only a few minutes to find the page that pictured the woman who looked so much like Jane. He turned on the copy machine and photocopied it. The black-and-white image that emerged from the machine didn't show the vivid color of the Minnesota nurse's hair, but that was imprinted on Herb's memory. As something of an art expert, he had an excellent memory for colors and shapes.

After the first sheet came out of the machine, he copied the pages that explained how house exchanging worked and gave hints for club members listed in the catalog, plus the page that listed the key for the codes used in the individual ads. When his job was completed, Herb folded his copies and put them into his pocket, then returned the catalog to Marlene's desk drawer.

He wasn't yet sure exactly how he would use these papers, but Herb had a hunch that they were going to help him with both of his problems—Jane and Kozlowski. As he returned to his desk and began to refine his thoughts into a game plan, he was relieved to realize that his headache was now completely gone.

As he locked up the gallery for the night, Herb Carmody began to feel that his run of sour luck was finally beginning to change.

6

"Soup ain't bad here," Sid Balzarian said. "I'm gonna have a bowl of that and a Caesar's, myself. Try to eat light at lunch." He patted his mid-section. On the short side at five feet six, he'd always been thin and wiry. But in middle age, Sid's muscle tone wasn't what it once had been and he could feel his youth slipping away from him. "Tryin' to keep in shape," he said. "But, hey Barry, don't let me stop ya, eat up. Whatever ya want, tab's on me this time."

Sid and Barry O'Farrell were at San Francisco's Stinking Rose Cafe, sitting at a window table where they could look out onto Columbus Avenue.

"Ain't they got nothin' here ain't full o' garlic?" Barry asked as he perused the menu. Unlike the smaller man across the table, Barry didn't believe in dieting and he had the bulk to prove it. He was six feet tall and he tipped the scales at two-thirty the first thing in the morning.

"That's the gimmick, pal. Garlic's the stinking rose, get it?" Barry shrugged his beefy shoulders. "Even got garlic ice cream for dessert, ya want some. What's the matter, ya don't like garlic?" Sid asked. He might have used a similar tone of voice to ask whether Barry had an aversion to sunny days or good sex.

"Sure, I like garlic fine, but I got a date tonight. Gonna stink the girl right outta my car, I show up after eatin' this stuff." Barry stroked his bristly brown mustache with his index finger. He'd grown it a few months ago in an attempt to draw attention away from his receding hairline. While Barry O'Farrell wasn't a bit self-conscious about his size, his approaching baldness troubled him immensely.

"Get the roast chicken, then," Sid suggested. "Pick off the garlic cloves, ya don't wanna eat 'em."

The waitress brought a basket of bread to their table, along with a plateful of roasted garlic and a bottle of olive oil. A few minutes later, Barry's bottle of Red Hook ale arrived. Sid stuck to iced tea, into which he mixed three packets of Sweet 'n Low. He had business to discuss and, for that, he wanted to be a hundred percent sober.

As he spread a thick paste of roasted garlic on a piece of bread, Sid leaned toward his lunch partner and lowered his voice. The loud din of conversation in the crowded Stinking Rose Cafe at noon would undoubtedly protect even a conversation held in normal tones from being overheard by anyone at a nearby table, but Sid wasn't taking any chances. "Look, Barry," he half-whispered. "I got this plan, see, and I need a reliable partner to pull it off, somebody's got balls."

Not about to deny he had balls, Barry swallowed his Red Hook and asked what Sid had in mind.

Sid leaned further forward. "There's this rich broad, see, I know her husband. Poor jerk's in up to his neck with his bookie, and this girl he's married to won't ante up two cents to bail him out." Sid tore off a section of bread with his teeth and chewed. The odor of his garlicky breath wafted toward Barry, who was dipping his own bread in the olive oil. "Ya see, Barry, I'm tryin' to be a friend to this guy, come up with a foolproof way to bail him outta his financial troubles and—"

"Talkin' about Herb Carmody, right?"

Sid's jaw sagged. He hadn't planned on telling Barry who his target was quite this early in the game, certainly not before his luncheon partner had actually signed on to the plan. Obviously, his description of the Carmodys had been too on target. Sid chewed and swallowed the last of his bread,

58

stealing a few moments to think. "Maybe it's Herb, maybe it ain't," he said finally.

"Let's assume it's somebody like Carmody, then," Barry said, taking a swig of ale straight from the bottle. "What ya got in mind?"

"Lemme ask ya somethin', Barry. Got anything against bendin' the law a little to help out a buddy? I mean, assumin' nobody gets hurt or nothin'."

The men's lunches arrived before Barry had a chance to answer. "How much bendin' you talking about here?" he asked after the waitress had retreated out of earshot. He used his fork to pierce the dozen or so garlic cloves nestled around his half chicken and transfer them to his bread plate.

"How much you willin' to bend?" His spoon poised above his steaming bowl of cream of garlic soup, Sid waited for the other man's answer.

"Depends how much it pays."

"Let's say a quarter mil, maybe closer to half a mil." Barry dropped his fork. It hit his plate with a loud ping. "Half a million *dollars?*"

"Keep your voice down," Sid ordered in a loud whisper. He looked around furtively, but no one in the crowd of young professionals on their lunch hours and tourists visiting a famous San Francisco attraction seemed to be paying any attention to their discussion.

"Half a million dollars?" Barry repeated. This time his question was barely audible to Sid.

"Heard you the first time," Sid said. "Our take could be in that neighborhood, dependin' on whether we have to cut anybody else in on this thing."

"Besides you 'n me 'n Herb."

"Assumin' it's Herb we're talking about."

"How much does Herb—I mean, your friend—get out of

this, assumin' me 'n you are gonna split a cool mil?"

Sid dipped his spoon into his soup and began to eat with loud slurping sounds. "Depends how much we decide to hand over," he said. "I mean, you and me, we'd be takin' most of the risks here, right? All this friend of mine's gotta do is collect the money from wherever his old lady's got it stashed and bring it to us. What he wants is to get out from under his bookie, right?" He licked his spoon clean and began waving it at Barry as he talked. "That's gonna cost a hundred grand, maybe a hundred and fifty, I'm not sure, depending on his interest rate. And what the hell, he oughta get a few bucks extra for makin' sure things go smooth. I'd say we give him one seventy-five, maybe two hundred tops."

Barry ripped the leg off his portion of chicken and began to gnaw on it. "Let's hear your scam."

Sid finished eating his soup and pushed his bowl away before he began to talk. "Way I see it, this rich broad'll only cut a check if it's to save her own skin, see? Won't give shit for her old man, so we can't play that angle. I figure once she gives the word to her bank or broker or whoever, the husband can get his hands on her money easy, no questions asked. Hubby bails her out, she thinks he's saved her ass, he gets to be a hero at home, see? He gets his share of the loot—she's got so much she don't even miss it—and my friend—well, he wins about six different ways."

"So what ya got in mind?"

As they finished eating their meals, Sid outlined the details of his plan to con Jane Parkhurst Carmody out of a cool million dollars. "So, you in or out?" Sid asked twenty minutes later, after he'd finished his pitch.

"Got one question first," Barry said, draining his second ale. "Let's stop playin' games about Herb Carmody. You 'n me both know who you're talkin' about."

"That ain't a question," Sid said.

"I'm gettin' to that. My question is, why ain't Herb sittin' here with us right now, plannin' this thing?"

Sid waited a moment before answering, then decided to take the plunge. If Barry wasn't coming in on this deal, it probably wasn't going to happen anyway. "Herb's a pussy, that's why," he said. "His idea of helpin' himself is sitting around Jocks gettin' drunk on a Sunday afternoon. When he ain't makin' more bad bets. We bring him in on this thing too early, he's gonna blow it for all of us."

Barry's face wore a puzzled expression. "I don't get it. When ya plannin' to clue him in?"

"When the time comes to collect," Sid said. "Then all he's gotta do is go to the bank or wherever his wife's got her dough stashed and deliver it to us. We give him his cut, he pays off his bookie and sets some aside for a rainy day or bets on the Giants games or whatever. Nobody gets hurt and we all got a helluva lot more money than we got now."

" 'Cept the rich wife."

"Fuck the rich wife."

"What if Herb don't go along? What if he says fuck you and calls the cops? What then?"

"You kiddin'? Herb owes a shitload o' money to Kozlowski and he ain't got it. Keeps kiddin' himself that he's gonna score big on some new wager, hit some kinda jackpot. Diggin' himself in deeper and deeper, that's all he's doin'. I tell ya, Barry, the guy's from Mars when it comes to street smarts. Not to mention he's fuckin' desperate."

"Kozlowski, huh?" Barry shook his head in amazement. "Real stupid move."

"That's what I mean about Herb. Man don't think ahead. So you 'n me, Barry, we're gonna do his thinkin' for him. When this thing goes down, Herb ain't gonna call no cops.

He's gonna kiss our asses from here till Sunday, he's gonna be so grateful."

"Lemme give it some thought," Barry said, using a piece of bread to sop up the last of his garlicky gravy. "Get back to you in a day or two." He shoved the bread into his mouth, chewed and swallowed, then pushed his chair away from the table.

"Hey, you ain't leavin', are ya?" Sid asked as Barry got to his feet. He was anxious to settle things now, not in a day or two.

"Got things to do."

"Ya mean you're not gonna stick around for some of that garlic ice cream?"

Barry rolled his eyes. "Probably blew my chance to score tonight as it is. They sell Clorets here?" As Barry passed Sid's chair, he clapped him on the shoulder. "Thanks for the lunch, Sid. Like I said, I'll get back to ya."

Sid watched as the larger man made his way to the other side of the crowded restaurant. Then he signaled the waitress for the check.

7

Claire moved the computer's mouse to "View Article" and clicked on it. In an instant, her computer screen was filled with newspaper features containing exactly the kind of statistical information she was seeking. She read article after article: "Calls to L.A. Domestic Abuse Hot Lines Soar;" "Victims Cross All Racial, Ethnic Lines;" "Secret Sojourn— In Santa Monica, Abused Women and Their Children Find a Haven and a Place to Start Over;" and half a dozen more.

Claire selected the articles she wanted to keep, clicked onto the print icon and glanced out the window while her laser printer whirred and the information from the *Los Angeles Times'* online archives was transformed into hard copy. It was almost dark outside now. The street lamps along Twentieth Street were coming on and traffic was increasing as people headed home from their jobs.

Taking the sheets from the printer, Claire read them over again. She planned to include some of the statistics gathered here in her article for *Glamour*, using them to lend perspective to her quotes from the battered women she'd interviewed at the shelters, and to the analysis and advice she'd gleaned from talking to several mental health experts.

An hour later, Claire was still at the computer keyboard, condensing the notes from one of her interviews into a few paragraphs about "Mary B.," a Northridge wife whose husband had slashed her throat with a butcher knife, leaving the poor woman with nothing more than a hoarse whisper for a voice. As she added Mary's grisly tale to her article, Claire could feel her shoulders becoming more and more tense.

What kind of man could take a knife to the throat of a woman he supposedly loved? she wondered. What kind of man could rape a woman he claimed to care for, or beat her, or throw acid in her face, even murder her? And what kind of woman stayed in a relationship with that kind of man, possibly until it was far, far too late?

What kind of mother could use her fists on her own daughter, turning the child into a human punching bag whenever she got drunk enough? And could that child ever fully recover from such violent beginnings?

Claire's research for this article had given her some of the answers to these complex questions, but certainly not all of them.

"Mary B. says she tried many times to escape her abusive home," Claire wrote, "but she explains in her hoarse whisper, 'Joe would always catch me before I made it around the corner. He would threaten to kill me and the kids if I didn't come back. I had to believe him.'

"But despite her return, Joe's violence continued to escalate and he took out more and more of his frustrations on the children, Mary now admits. One day, when she tried to step between her husband and their eight-year-old son to protect the youngster, everything came to a head. Joe went berserk, grabbed a knife from the kitchen and—"

Her eyes misting up as she stared at the computer screen, Claire had to stop writing for a few minutes. She knew she was in danger of losing her usual journalist's distance and perspective on this article. As she wrote about Mary and Joe and their two traumatized children, all her own personal terrors came rushing back. The way she'd felt each time Mama's razor tongue sliced into her and cut out a piece of her psyche. The many, many times she'd thrown herself between Mama and Ellen, doing her best to protect her little sister.

Even the primitive fear she'd felt just last night, when Charlie pounded his fists against her door, cursing her because she'd changed the locks and refused to let him in.

"You don't live here anymore!" Claire'd screamed at him through the locked door. What did he expect, after the way he so cruelly destroyed her manuscript and her books—that she'd make it easy for him to come into her home again? "Stay the hell away, bastard!"

But Claire wasn't sure Charlie had even heard her retort, he'd been making such a racket with his fists. At first, what frightened her most was the chance that her landlord would hear Charlie and use the commotion as an excuse to evict her from her little rent-controlled sanctuary. But after spending all day combing through her notes for her article on spousal abuse, she began to wonder whether eviction from her apartment might not be the least of her potential worries.

Unlike Claire's mother, who for more than a year before her death from cirrhosis was almost constantly drunk, Charlie was a periodic binge drinker. When he'd had too much, Charlie often flew into a rage, but so far he'd never taken out his anger on Claire—at least not physically. A few months after their wedding, the very first time she witnessed one of his temper tantrums, she'd warned him that she would never again put up with being struck—by anybody. And her husband had never touched her in anger. Even when he was drunk, he'd somehow managed not to cross that line.

Instead, Charlie took out his frustrations on inanimate objects. He punched holes in the plasterboard walls, broke dishes, yanked more than one door off its hinges, pounded dents into the roof of his car. The next day, hung over but contrite, he always took out his toolbox and tried his best to repair the damage he'd done.

Still, Claire knew, every batterer had a first time. And now she was pushing Charlie farther than ever before.

Cut it out, she told herself. *You're letting your imagination run wild because of this goddamned article.* She simply was identifying too closely with the unfortunate women she'd interviewed. After all, Charlie was no Joe B. He would never attack his wife with a knife. Her husband's problem was just that he turned into a two-year-old brat when he'd had a few too many. Claire had nothing to fear from Charlie. Really she didn't.

Claire glanced at the clock. It was after seven. She decided she'd worked hard enough for today. Besides, she needed a chance to clear her head before finishing this assignment if she was going to give *Glamour* her usual professional job. After filing her partial article, she backed it up on a floppy disk and shut off her computer.

As she rose from her chair, Claire glanced out the window once more. With a sharp intake of breath, she recognized a car parked across the street. The glow of the street lamp accentuated the dents in the roof of Charlie's old burgundy Accord.

Was he coming back here? Claire braced herself for a replay of last night's unpleasantness and made a silent vow not to open the door to him, no matter what. She shut off her office lights and stood in the dark for a time, looking out the window at the parked car. Now she could see someone sitting in the driver's seat of the Honda, watching her apartment.

When, after ten minutes, Charlie McVee still had not gotten out of his car and headed across the street, Claire began to believe that he didn't intend to.

Tonight, he was simply watching. And waiting.

Ellen Merchant rolled over in bed and squinted at the alarm clock on the nightstand. It was nearly three o'clock, time to get up. As she yawned and stretched, she could hear children's voices in the street outside as they made their way home from school.

Despite a full seven hours of sleep, Ellen still felt tired. She was having trouble getting used to her relatively new upside down life of working nights and sleeping days. Last night had been a particularly difficult one, too, with Gladys Edmonds suffering another minor heart attack. Ellen had given her patient the appropriate emergency care, then called for an ambulance and accompanied her to the hospital. If the old woman suffered no more setbacks, she would be allowed to return home today, in time for Ellen's night shift duties. But it was obvious that Mrs. Edmonds was moving closer to death.

As a nurse, Ellen had seen many people die. But when she worked in the hospital, she seldom got to know her patients as well as she did her private duty charges. The many hours she and Mrs. Edmonds had spent together made the old woman's impending death a great deal harder for her to accept.

Ellen slipped into her yellow chenille robe and headed for the kitchen to make a pot of coffee. After putting two leftover bran muffins in the toaster oven to reheat for breakfast, she retrieved her morning newspaper and the day's mail.

Nibbling on the first of the muffins, Ellen leafed through her day's mail—this month's bill from Dayton's department store, another from Minnegasco, two political ads for the upcoming election, this week's *Time*, and three personal letters.

Ellen did not recognize the names of any of the people who had written to her, but she felt a little flash of excitement as she saw that the first was postmarked Honolulu, Hawaii. Envisioning herself swimming in a warm tropical sea a few weeks hence, maybe even meeting an exciting new man while on vacation, she eagerly tore open the envelope, and read:

Dear Miss Merchant,

Thank you for your enticing letter regarding a possible house exchange for my Hawaii home later this year. Unfortunately, your proposal does not fit into my travel plans at this time, but I wish you luck in finding someone who wishes to visit your fine town.

It was signed by Mr. Henry Umecki. At least Mr. Umecki had taken the time to reply to her letter, Ellen told herself as a strong wave of disappointment washed over her. Most of the club members she'd queried simply ignored her letters if they had no interest in swapping homes with her.

The second letter, this one postmarked Scottsdale, Arizona, contained more of the same; this time, however, the writer was far blunter. In neatly typewritten words, Ellen's correspondent wrote that she and her husband "couldn't foresee any circumstances under which we would choose to vacation in Minnesota, now or in the future. However, we do appreciate your interest in our home."

"Damn," Ellen muttered under her breath as she dropped both letters into the wastebasket she kept underneath the sink, then poured herself a fresh cup of coffee before opening the third, which had a Duluth postmark. Her bare feet felt cold against the blue linoleum floor and a shiver ran down her spine. Soon the Twin Cities weather would turn colder and the icy north winds would usher in another frigid winter. Fall had definitely arrived.

Warming her hands around her coffee mug, Ellen gazed out the kitchen window. Across the street, half a dozen grade-school-age children were collecting fallen leaves from neighbors' lawns into one gigantic pile. When their brown-and-orange leaf mound had grown deep enough, they began taking turns jumping off a front porch railing into it. Shrieking with delight, they belly-flopped or curled into a ball and propelled themselves off the porch, landing squarely in the center of the leaves, breathless but unhurt.

Ellen smiled, remembering doing the same thing when she was a child living on this block. When winter came, she knew, the same children would build snow forts and go skating on an ice rink that somebody's father would build in his backyard.

For the very young, the bitter cold was an adventure. But, for her, it had long ago lost most of its magic. When winter arrived, Ellen wondered, would she still be here in her kitchen, drinking hot coffee and dreaming of warmer climes, wishing she were in the middle of some romantic sojourn in a faraway place?

There was always Claire's place, she reminded herself. Ellen knew she was always welcome to spend a week at her sister's apartment in Santa Monica. But she'd done that each year for the past three and it was no longer her idea of a real vacation.

Claire always seemed to be off somewhere interviewing somebody, or holed up in her home office writing a freelance article, while Ellen spent her days driving the nerve-wracking Los Angeles freeways or walking the beaches alone. Nights, Ellen slept on the sofa in the living room of Claire's small apartment.

A big advantage this year, of course, would be that Charlie McVee would no longer be there. Because of Claire and Charlie's pending divorce, Ellen would no longer have to put up with her brother-in-law's intrusion into every conversation she tried to have with her sister.

On the other hand, Claire no longer owned a sofa. This year, Ellen would probably have to sleep on the floor.

Ellen truly wanted to spend time with her older sister, particularly because she sensed that Claire sorely needed her support during this difficult time in her life. Maybe if she went to Los Angeles, she could talk with Charlie, get him to stop watching Claire's apartment, stalking her, all those things Claire'd told her he'd been doing lately. Yet Ellen knew that if she went to Los Angeles, she and her sister were likely to have little real time together. If things went as usual, Claire would never stop working as long as she was at home.

No, Ellen thought, she needed to lure Claire away somewhere, to someplace where she wouldn't be able to escape into her constant work, particularly now. To someplace where she wouldn't have to worry about looking out the window and finding Charlie McVee sitting there, watching her every move. Ellen had recognized the fear in her sister's voice when they'd last talked. She knew Claire needed a break, a change of scenery at least as much as she did.

Ellen carried her coffee back to the table and tore open the third envelope, the one with the Duluth return address. It sparked none of the excitement in her heart that the Hawaii and Arizona ones had. As she read the letter, Ellen began to understand how some of the people she'd written to must have felt when they received her correspondence.

The message was polite and to the point. The writer was a Duluth librarian who had read Ellen's entry in the house exchange catalog. Would Ellen consider spending four or five days vacationing in Duluth this November while the librarian attended a convention in Minneapolis? Ellen remembered seeing the librarian's listing in the exchange book . . . and choosing to ignore it. It had been one of the very few ads requesting a house exchange in the Twin Cities. If only Ellen had the least desire to go to Duluth . . . If only Duluth were the kind of place that would entice Claire to vacation with her . . .

Feeling depressed, Ellen wondered whether house exchanging was inherently destined to work out this way, where what one person wanted never seemed to jibe with someone else's desires. Did people ever manage to make arrangements where both parties ended up feeling thrilled by a new opportunity?

Ellen decided not to throw away the Duluth librarian's letter. The woman deserved an answer. Ellen would simply wait a few days, maybe a week. By then, she hoped to know for certain whether she could do better.

If no one responded to her own mailings, Ellen told herself, at least Duluth would be something different, and it wouldn't cost much. She could drive there in a few hours for the price of a tank full of gas. She hadn't been to Duluth since she was a child, and it might be better than visiting Claire again this year. At least, in the Duluth house, she told herself, she would have a real bed to sleep in.

Ellen tucked the librarian's letter into the kitchen drawer where she kept her grocery lists and her unpaid bills. By this time next week, she would make her decision. Duluth, Los Angeles, or simply staying home.

Unless, as Ellen fervently hoped, someplace warm and exciting, someplace she—and, she hoped, Claire as well—had never been before suddenly became one of the choices.

8

"My wife had to make an emergency trip to care for her mother," Herb said as he handed over the withdrawal slip and Jane's certificate of deposit, which he had taken from the safe deposit box yesterday. "Got the call late last night. Her mother had a major stroke and Jane had to grab the first flight she could get. You know what that's like—takes time to find a good nursing home. Not to mention plenty of money."

Anne Clark, a First Security Bank assistant vice president, muttered a few words of condolence. A forty-plus woman in a severely cut navy suit that she hoped would hide her rather large bosom, her best physical asset was her kind face. Herb had selected her from among the bank's officers on duty today because she looked motherly, understanding, and significantly more gullible than the others.

"Jane was sure the bank would help with our unexpected little problem," Herb continued, speaking in confidential tones, as if to an old, old friend. "Since we've banked with you for so long, we hoped you could bend the rules a little . . . just this once."

"Well, it's always better if the person whose name is on the C.D. cashes it—"

"Of course, and we never dreamed we'd have to cash it in early, but you know what nursing homes cost nowadays." Herb's face registered regret while, out of Anne Clark's view, he wiped his sweaty palms against the knees of his gray wool slacks.

The bank officer briefly examined the documents Herb had brought. "I'll see what I can do," she said with an encouraging smile. "Just wait here a minute. I'll be right back."

Herb watched out of the corner of his eye as Anne Clark walked around the oak-paneled tellers' counter of the Tiburon branch bank. He held his breath as she pulled open a drawer in a wooden cabinet much like the ones libraries use for their card catalogs and compared the signature he'd carefully forged on the withdrawal slip with Jane's on the original signature card. After the woman had closed the drawer again, apparently satisfied that the signatures matched, he began to breathe normally once more. He was pleased to see that she didn't reach for the telephone, although he'd been prepared to have the bank try to call Jane to confirm his story that she'd taken an emergency flight out of town this morning.

There was no chance his wife would actually answer the phone, of course; Herb had made sure of that. Jane had a meeting of her hospital auxiliary entertainment committee in San Francisco this afternoon. He'd come home for lunch and watched her leave the house more than two hours ago.

"You understand that there's a penalty for early withdrawal, Mr. Carmody?" Anne asked when she returned to her desk.

Herb nodded. "Tough break, but no nursing home is going to wait for a CD to mature, right? They want their money up front."

Anne punched some figures into her desktop computer. "After subtracting the penalty, the balance in the account is fifteen thousand three hundred twelve dollars and seventeen cents."

The amount was a few hundred dollars short of what Herb had anticipated, but he was in no position to argue. This was the largest certificate of deposit Jane had kept in the safe deposit box and he'd been afraid to cash in more than one of them; he would have to settle for what he could get. He knew she had a few larger ones in the metal box on her closet shelf, but she'd be much more likely to notice one of them was missing. "I'd like a cashier's check for that amount, please," he said.

"How about if I just transfer it right into Mrs. Carmody's checking account here at First Security?" Anne suggested.

"No, thanks," Herb said, trying to keep his manner casual. "Just make out the check to Jane Carmody and I'll send it on to her."

The last thing Herb wanted was for this money to end up in Jane's personal checking account, where he'd have a devil of a time getting his hands on it again. But from past experience, he knew he would have no trouble depositing this cashier's check into the checking account he and Jane held jointly at First Federal, even without her endorsing it. Then he could write his own checks to withdraw the money again.

Five minutes later, Herb left First Security Bank with the cashier's check tucked into the inside pocket of his tweed sport jacket. He walked down the main street of town and promptly deposited it into the joint checking account at the Tiburon branch of First Federal. Jane had been keeping only a few hundred dollars in this account ever since the fiasco with the ten-thousand-dollar check, but now it was flush again. After he deposited the check, Herb drove across the bridge into San Francisco, where he visited two more First Federal branches.

At the branch offices, he cashed checks for seventy-five hundred and seventy-eight hundred dollars, respectively, taking the money in fifty- and hundred-dollar bills.

By the time the banks had closed and Jane's committee had voted for a magician to entertain the kids on the surgical ward, Herb had made another stop, to pay off another chunk of his debt with Kozlowski. It didn't seem to make much difference to his debt, however—the interest the shark was charging him seemed to eat up most of any payment he made. Then he headed for Waves.

"Take the rest of the afternoon off," he told Ginny, his acting manager at the Jefferson Street gallery. "Beautiful day. Go enjoy it." The shop was empty of customers and no new inventory had arrived today, so there was little for Ginny to do, anyway.

"Hey, thanks, Herb," Ginny said, her face lighting up at the prospect of found time. "You can be a real sweetheart sometimes." Twenty-four-year-old Ginny Wu had worked at Waves for the past four months, ever since her graduation from San Francisco State University. This was her first salaried job and she sorely missed the relative freedom of her student life now that she was chained to Waves for eight hours a day. Being offered the rest of the afternoon off was an unexpected and valuable bonus.

"Nothing here I can't handle by myself," Herb told her, pleased by his employee's visible gratitude.

Alone in the shop a few minutes later, Herb put the CLOSED sign on the front door and headed for the back room, running his fingers over the smooth wooden surface of a hand-carved humpback whale as he passed it. Taking the pages he'd copied from Marlene LeBaron's house exchange catalog out of his briefcase, he rolled a sheet of paper into the typewriter on Ginny's desk and began to write to the pretty redheaded nurse whose photograph had caught his eye.

Herb knew there was no question he had to do something soon to bail himself out of the financial and personal morass he was in. He was being pushed hard, too hard—from both sides. He'd now pawned several more pieces of Jane's jewelry to place bets or make payments on his debt and, after this morning's performance at the bank, there was simply no going back. Jane would not just divorce him; she would turn him in to the cops and insist that he be prosecuted for theft or forgery or fraud or whatever else she could add to his list of crimes against her.

Yet, Herb knew, if he hadn't come up with that payment for Kozlowski today, the consequences would have been even more severe. If he didn't get out from under soon, he'd be a dead man. If Kozlowski didn't kill him, surely a heart attack in prison would.

The way Herb saw it, Jane was both his problem and his solution. If she was out of the way for good—purportedly out of town somewhere on an extended trip—he could continue to siphon off her money, just as he had today. Cashing in that CD had filled him with newfound self-confidence, and it was only the beginning. There was plenty more where that came from—CD's, hefty stock dividend checks that arrived frequently in the mail, Jane's other bank accounts, bonds that were due to mature in the next few months, her remaining jewelry. Once he got his hands on Jane's income, he could pay off Kozlowski in full and start all over again before the beginning of basketball season.

What Herb was planning pricked his conscience, he had to admit. After all, he and Jane went way back together—he could remember her as a skinny, freckle-faced, carrot-topped ninth grader who came to all their Santa Barbara high school swim meets. He'd been a senior in those days, and his claim to fame was the first place trophy he'd won at the statewide high school swimming competition. Jane was incredibly impressed with him. So was the scout from USC, who'd offered Herb a full scholarship to the university if he would simply compete on its swim team and maintain a C average in his classes.

Herb and Jane hadn't married until ten years after Herb

won his last high school swim meet, though—well after he'd bombed out of the Olympic qualifying trials, finished his college degree, and discovered he didn't much like working for a living—at least not working for anybody but himself. As Herb considered his options, he decided that marrying Jane would be the easiest way to live the good life he so coveted.

Unfortunately, it hadn't taken long for him to discover he'd been dead wrong about that. Marrying for money turned out to be the hardest way Herb had ever earned a dollar.

Herb didn't think of what he was planning as murder; murder was cold, violent, something done by criminals, not by somebody like Herbert Carmody, a man who'd almost been an Olympian. He was merely evening the odds, finding a way to survive. Jane had brought this on herself, really. If she'd shared with him the way he'd had to share with her, none of this would be necessary. The tricky part, he figured, would be getting rid of Jane without casting suspicion on himself. That's where Ellen Merchant, the Minnesota nurse came in.

There was a phone number printed beneath the Merchant woman's photo. Herb supposed it would be all right to phone her, but he preferred to accompany his sales pitch with some visual aids, so he decided to put it in writing. He typed efficiently, choosing his words with care and, when he'd finished his letter, he slid it into a red-white-and-blue cardboard mailer. He added two color photos of the Tiburon house, then dropped the slender package into the Federal Express box down the street. Nurse Ellen would receive his query tomorrow morning.

If she responded as Herb fervently hoped she would, the first step of his master plan would be in place.

Sid Balzarian drove his old Chevrolet up the hill past the

Carmody house, then turned around where the road came to a dead end at the summit. He hardly noticed the panoramic view of San Francisco Bay and the city skyline beyond from this deserted cul de sac, which was a favorite nighttime hangout for amorous local teenagers. Sid wasn't here to enjoy the scenery; he wanted to get a better look at Jane Carmody and begin to learn her habits. When the time came to implement his plan, he wanted to make sure he and Barry O'Farrell made no foolish mistakes.

Sid pulled off the road just below the Carmodys' place and waited. This morning, unlike yesterday and the day before, he was in luck. Less than half an hour after he'd parked his car, Jane's dark green Jaguar pulled out of her driveway and passed him. He could see that the woman behind the wheel had a mop of bright red hair and that she was alone in the car.

Jane Carmody was driving, Sid was certain. He'd gotten a quick glimpse of her that night he'd driven the drunken Herb home from San Francisco. A good-looking babe wearing an electric blue satin strapless dress, she'd looked like she was on her way to some sort of fancy dress ball.

But what Sid remembered most from that night, apart from the Carmody broad's obvious displeasure with her husband's inebriated condition, was her hair. A mass of curls that reached halfway down her bare back, it was the same bright copper color as Rusty, the golden retriever Sid had owned as a kid. Now, with the morning sunlight pouring through the Jaguar's open sunroof, Jane's hair was so red it seemed almost to be on fire.

Sid sank down in the front seat of the Chevy until the Carmody woman got a couple of hundred yards past where he was parked. Then he started his engine and followed her down the hill into town.

As she drove, Jane Carmody's foot was heavy on the accelerator, as though she was late for an important appointment. Sid watched as she slid straight through a stop sign into an intersection, just ahead of the Ford station wagon that had the legal right of way. The Ford's driver slammed on his brakes, then tapped his horn in protest. Jane appeared momentarily startled, but recovered quickly and waved an apology at the other driver through her Jaguar's open sunroof.

"Bitch is in some kinda hurry," Sid said, sympathizing with the station wagon's rattled driver. When his own turn came, he sped through the intersection, worried that his old bucket of bolts wouldn't be able to keep up with the Jag if the Carmody broad headed for the freeway. Not the way she was driving.

But Sid was in luck. Jane headed away from the freeway, straight into the town of Tiburon, where she took a right turn into the street that ran along the edge of the Bay. Just beyond a row of shops selling music boxes, historic photographs, and T-shirts advertising Tiburon, she took another right turn into an hourly-rate parking lot.

Sid drove on past, pulling his Chevy into the first parking spot he found on the street. The curb was green, indicating that it was a twenty-minute zone.

By the time Jane had locked up her Jag and was sprinting across the parking lot toward the ferry station, Sid was standing in front of the Swedish cafe across the street, watching her from behind his mirrored sunglasses. He stayed where he was until Herb's wife, in her custom-made teal green trench coat, was half a block ahead and a group of elderly tourists getting off a charter bus began to block his view.

Pushing his way though the sea of white hair and polyester pants suits, Sid hurried until he spotted Jane once more. With a sigh of relief, he saw that she was now on the dock with the crowd boarding the ten o'clock ferry to San Francisco.

There was no need to follow Jane Carmody any farther today, Sid decided, no reason to risk her catching on that he'd been following her. Even from a hundred feet away, he had no trouble picking Jane Carmody out of the gathering on the dock. The woman's long red hair shone like a neon sign and, in bright daylight, it was every bit as visible.

As the ferry's whistle tooted three times to signal its pending departure, Sid turned and headed back toward his old Chevy. As he reached the curb, he saw the local parking cop making her way down the street, looking for chalk marks she'd put earlier on the tires of parked cars and writing an occasional ticket. He walked faster.

Sid had done a good morning's work, but he wasn't satisfied yet. If he and Barry were going to pull this one off successfully, he knew all the pieces of his plan had to fit together with precision.

As Sid pulled the Chevy away from the curb just ahead of the parking cop's arrival, he checked off another item on his mental list of things to do. Next was to take a fresh look at his late Uncle Edwin's house outside Petaluma.

As Sid drove out of town toward Highway 101, he was careful to keep his speed below the legal limit.

9

The doorbell woke Ellen from a deep sleep. She looked at the bedside clock through bleary eyes; it was ten in the morning and she'd been in bed for only two hours. Groggily, she grabbed her robe from the bedside chair and pushed her arms into its sleeves.

It had better not be anybody selling anything, she thought, thoroughly irritated. Ever since she'd begun working nights, Ellen had developed a hatred for the solicitors who frequently interrupted her day's sleep, either by telephone or showing up at her door.

The doorbell chimed once more before Ellen made it out of the bedroom. She dragged herself to the front door and peered through the small round window in its center just in time to see the back of a young man retreating toward the Federal Express truck parked at the curb. In his hand was a slender red, white and blue package.

Ellen pushed open the door. A notice of an attempt to make a delivery fell off the outside handle of the door and landed at her feet. "Hey!" she called. "Come back here, I'm home."

The deliveryman turned around and headed back toward Ellen. As he spotted her robe and disheveled hair, his round acne-scarred face took on a look of embarrassment. "Sorry if I woke you," he told her. "Delivery for Ellen Merchant."

"That's me. I work nights, so I have to sleep during the daytime." Lately, whenever anyone other than a door-to-door salesperson showed up at her door during daylight hours, Ellen felt compelled to explain why she'd been sleeping. The thought that a visitor might conclude she was merely lazy disturbed her a great deal. She'd always prided herself on being responsible, a hard worker. What other people thought of her mattered to Ellen, undoubtedly far more than it should—another result of growing up in a dysfunctional family, she'd since learned.

"Sign here, please." The Federal Express driver handed Ellen the flat package and she signed for it. With a quick nod of his head, he hurried back to his truck.

Ellen closed the door and, rubbing her reddened eyes, dropped onto a soft living room chair. Receiving a special delivery like this one was an unusual event in her life.

Despite her heavy fatigue, she was far too curious about the contents of the cardboard mailer to set it aside until she'd completed her necessary seven hours of sleep. She tore it open and stuck her hand inside.

Ellen inspected the two photographs the mailer held first; they showed a big driftwood gray wood-and-glass house perched high on a hill above a wide body of water. As she read the neatly typed letter that accompanied the snapshots, her heartbeat began to quicken with excitement. The vacation she'd dreamed about was going to happen, she thought, a broad smile breaking across her weary face; it actually was going to happen, despite all the turndowns to her letters that she'd received in the past few days.

To Ellen, the house in the photographs seemed like something straight out of *House Beautiful*. The letter explained that it was located in a village called Tiburon, California, across San Francisco Bay from the city. She'd heard of Tiburon and guessed that it was not far from the more famous tourist attraction of Sausalito.

Her need for sleep set aside for the moment, Ellen grabbed her road atlas, opened it to the map of California, and located

Tiburon. She was right; the town was in Marin County, immediately north of San Francisco. From what she could see here, San Francisco was probably only about half an hour's drive away from Tiburon, across the Golden Gate Bridge.

Ellen had never been to northern California and the prospect of going there now quickly began to intrigue her. The letter said that this house had two bedrooms and three bathrooms, along with a panoramic view of the bay and the San Francisco skyline. The miracle was that Herbert Carmody, the man who had written to Ellen, and his wife were apparently willing to trade a week in this wonderful house for a week at her much more modest place. Their offer seemed almost too good to be true.

Ellen glanced at the antique clock on the fireplace mantle and realized that it was still early in California, well before nine o'clock. The phone number Herbert Carmody had given her was the one for his business, an art gallery called Waves II. Would he be at work this early in the day? Too excited to wait, she grabbed for the telephone and dialed the West Coast. When a machine answered at the art gallery, she quickly hung up. She didn't want to leave a recorded message, then have to worry all day about when Mr. Carmody might call her back.

Instead, Ellen went into the kitchen and made herself a pot of raspberry herbal tea. She sat at the round oak kitchen table, drinking the warm brew and trying the California phone number every few minutes.

While she waited for her correspondent to arrive at his gallery, Ellen also called her travel agent and checked on airfares to San Francisco, then got out her two house exchange catalogs and tried to look up the Carmodys. She didn't find them in either book, but that meant little. It had been a full six months after she joined the club before her own first ad appeared. As she sipped her second cup of tea, Ellen progressed to making a list of clothes she would pack for her trip west.

By the time a man finally answered the telephone at Waves II, Ellen Merchant was mentally prepared to get on the next plane headed for the West Coast.

"Waves II," he said.

Once Ellen was certain she was speaking with Herbert Carmody, she identified herself. "I just got your letter, Mr. Carmody, and the pictures, too, and I'm definitely interested in a house exchange if we can arrange a schedule that's good for both of us." She felt a little breathless with anticipation, but did her best to sound cool and rational.

"I'm glad to hear that, Ms. Merchant," Herb told her. "I'd really like to make the trip as soon as possible." He went on to explain that his gallery specialized in marine art and that he'd been anxious to meet with a few Midwestern artists whose work he'd admired. "We're thinking about expanding into freshwater art at Waves."

"My schedule's pretty flexible," Ellen said, nervously sketching a picture of a duck in flight on the edge of the packing list she'd made. "I work as a private duty nurse, on call, and I only have to give my agency a few days' notice to get time off."

"Think you might be able to come, say, a week from Sunday?"

Ellen glanced at the glossy calendar hanging on the wall of her kitchen. It had been a gift from Claire and it featured reproductions of paintings by nearly forgotten women artists. "The eighth?" she asked.

"Right. I figure we can both travel on Sunday. That way, I'll be able to get right down to business first thing Monday morning."

"I think that will work for me." Ellen made a note of the

date. "I'm curious, though. How come you picked my place?" What she really wanted to know was why the Carmodys would be willing to swap their obviously superior home for her tiny bungalow, but she didn't want to jeopardize the deal by putting her question quite that bluntly.

Herb Carmody's laugh echoed over the line. "It's stupid, I know," he told Ellen, "but I have this thing about hotels—I absolutely hate them. So when a friend told me about this house exchange thing, it sounded great. I don't know if you looked in the catalog—"

"Yes, I did."

"Anyway, my wife and I, we just signed up with the club. That's why we're not listed yet."

"This is my first time in the book myself."

"The thing is, we saw your photo and thought you looked like a nice young woman. Jane, my wife, is pretty picky, I'm afraid. She doesn't want anybody who smokes or has children or pets or anything like that using our place, and she liked the fact you're a nurse."

"I can see why she'd want to be careful," Ellen said, her eyes drawn once again to the photographs of the Carmodys' posh house.

"Truth is, there aren't that many places to pick from in Minneapolis and St. Paul, either, especially after you rule out all the smokers and pet owners and such. And there was one other thing that attracted us to your listing."

"What's that?"

"That there's only you."

"Only me?"

"Right. I mean, with just one person staying here, especially a professional nurse like you, we figured we wouldn't have to worry about our home being left dirty or damaged, right?"

Ellen stiffened. She knew she should stop right now, before anything was finalized, and ask Mr. Carmody for permission to bring her sister along. Would he and his wife really refuse to swap houses if she told them there would be two people involved?

But something held Ellen back from being totally honest. She didn't even know if Claire would be able to make it, she rationalized. Why should she risk losing this dream vacation over such a small thing? She could always bring up the subject later.

"I—I'm a very clean person," Ellen said finally, "and I promise I'll treat your home just like my own."

"So we're all set, then? For the eighth?"

Ellen was slightly taken aback. She'd expected more bargaining back and forth before both sides agreed to an exchange. But this Carmody fellow clearly believed in nailing things down quickly. Perhaps, as a businessman, he was used to making decisions and finalizing deals in a hurry. "I—I'd better check with my agency first," she said, "and make sure I can get a plane reservation. But I'm sure it'll be all right. Just let me make a couple of calls and I'll get back to you this afternoon."

"Oh," Herb said, "there's just one more thing. If you could do us a favor, we'd really appreciate it."

"What kind of favor?"

"I assume you have a driver's license."

"Sure. Why?"

"We'd like to leave our car in the short-term parking lot at San Francisco International Airport. We'll leave the keys and the parking receipt, along with directions telling you where to find it, at your airline's ticket counter inside the terminal. If you could just drive it home for us, it would save us having to hire a cab. You know how they are—they tend to be so unreliable these days."

"I—I s'pose I could do that. What kind of car is it?"

"A Jaguar. But don't worry, it has an automatic transmission. You won't have any trouble driving it."

A Jaguar! Ellen couldn't believe that this man was actually asking her to drive a car worth as much as she might earn in two years of private duty nursing. "I don't— Are you really sure you want me driving your car?"

"Unless it's too much trouble. Actually, please feel free to use the Jag during the week you're staying at our house as well. You'll need a car to get into town and there's no sense in your having to rent one. Then you can just drop the Jag back at the airport for us when you fly out again."

"Well, sure, I mean I'd love to. I—I guess you could use my car here, too, but it's nothing special, just a ninety-four Honda Civic."

"Thanks, Ms. Merchant, but that's not really necessary. I expect I'll hire a car and driver to take me around the Twin Cities while we're there. I'm pretty bad at reading maps. If you want to leave your car keys at your house, though, maybe Jane would like to use your Honda around town while I'm off working."

"Sure, that'd be fine. Save all of us a lot of money, right? I mean—" Ellen felt foolish the minute the words had left her mouth. Obviously the Carmodys weren't the slightest bit worried about saving money, not with that fantastic house of theirs and a Jaguar to drive, plus a hired car and driver whenever they took a trip. She was embarrassed that she'd alluded to how carefully she had to watch every penny, not to mention worried that Herbert Carmody and his wife might have second thoughts about whether her modest home would really be good enough for them.

"So, you think you can let me know later today then?" Herb asked.

87

Ellen was relieved that her slip of the tongue about saving money apparently hadn't put the man off. "Just as soon as I talk to my boss and my travel agent," she promised.

After she'd hung up the telephone, Ellen sat at the kitchen table for a few minutes, staring at the calendar on the wall, a broad smile on her freckled face. She could hardly believe her good fortune. A whole week in gorgeous, exclusive Tiburon. A Jaguar to drive. A golden opportunity to spend a whole week living a life of luxury, just like rich people!

She made a plane reservation with no trouble at all and, immediately afterward, as she dialed Better Home Care's telephone number to tell her supervisor not to schedule her to work during the week of the eighth, she felt suddenly energized, fully alive. An hour later, after she'd called Herb Carmody back to confirm their plans for the exchange, Ellen climbed back into bed.

But now she was far too excited by her pending adventure to fall back asleep.

Claire was on her hands and knees, removing the yellowed wax from the worn kitchen floor with a brush and an old, dull paring knife, when the telephone on the wall rang. She stiffened apprehensively, making no move to answer it. Instead, she dropped the scrub brush back into the suds-filled plastic bucket, stood up, and wiped off her wet hands on the back of her denim shorts.

By the time the phone rang for the fourth time, Claire was in her office, listening for her caller's message on her answering machine.

When her short recorded greeting ended and the beep sounded, a familiar-sounding woman's voice said, "Oh, dammit, Claire, I was really hoping I'd catch you at home."

Claire grabbed the receiver and clicked off the answering

machine. "Hi, Ellen, I'm here. Just letting the machine screen my calls these days."

"Oh, good," Claire's sister said. "I mean, I'm glad you're home, but— What's the matter? Charlie still giving you trouble?"

"Like I told you the other day, the jerk's been calling here five or six times a day to dump on me about something or other. When he's not parked across the street, staring at my windows, that is. It's a lot easier just not to talk to him." Claire plopped down onto her desk chair. Her back ached and her knees were bright red from kneeling for the past hour on the hard kitchen floor. At least her current discomfort was entirely physical, however. She found it far easier to take than the emotional pain Charlie was managing to inflict on her. "What's up?" she asked.

"You're not going to believe this," Ellen said, the excitement in her voice clearly evident. "I've arranged the most wonderful house exchange for next week. It's absolutely perfect."

"That's great, Ellie. I'm happy for you. Where are you going?"

"To Tiburon, right across the bay from San Francisco. Ever been there?"

Claire thought for a moment. "Once, I think, maybe ten, eleven years ago, just for lunch or something. I can remember taking the ferry over from San Francisco." She massaged her sore knees with her free hand while she talked. "Hey, El, think you might be able to stop off in L.A. on your way there or your way back home? I sure would love to see you."

"Got a better idea, Claire—you come to Tiburon with me. We both need a vacation."

"What? But I've got my article for *Glamour* to finish and—" Claire's words came as a reflex action. These days she thought of herself as too busy and too broke to think about taking vacations. And when she wasn't working, she was smack in the middle of her new project—removing every physical trace of Charlie McVee from her apartment.

"Don't give me that, Claire," Ellen said. "Of course you can come with me."

"But—"

"I don't want to hear any of your buts this time. I bet you don't have one really good reason you can't get away for a few days. I mean, for god's sake, you don't even have to buy an airline ticket to go to Tiburon. You can drive there in—what, five or six hours? And everything else will be completely free, so don't try telling me you can't afford it."

"I—it does sound tempting. But next week? It's so soon and I have this deadline for *Glamour*. I've got to get another assignment pretty quick, too, if I want to keep paying my rent."

"So write a travel article about Tiburon or San Francisco or something. Or do a piece on house exchanging. Something cheerful for a change. Come on, Claire, give us both a break, will you? I've got this all set up and I'm counting on you. The keys to this great house already came in today's mail, and I've bought my plane tickets and everything."

"Look, hon," Claire said, glancing out her office window at the sidewalk outside. There was nobody there, and Charlie's Accord was nowhere in sight. If she went away for a few days, she wondered, would her husband try to break in here? "The truth is, I'm kind of afraid to go away and leave my apartment empty right now. What if Charlie—"

"Thought you said you changed the locks."

"I did, but you know what Charlie can be like. He'll do just about anything to bug me these days. It's like he's got some kind of weird vendetta against me." Late at night, when she lay alone in her bed, Claire often thought about how she could have been married to Charlie McVee for so many years, yet never have realized he could be so mean and petty toward her. She'd seen him treat other people that way, of course, but she'd kidded herself that she was the exception, that he could never turn on her. How could she have been so blind? She hadn't yet come up with a satisfactory explanation.

"So ask your landlord to watch out for Charlie and call the cops if he tries anything, all right?" Ellen sighed with open exasperation. "Listen, Claire, I don't want to sound cruel here, but are you going to live the rest of your life waiting to react to whatever shit your husband pulls on you? Or are you going to start living your own life?"

Claire bit her lower lip hard to stop it from quivering. She always felt so close to tears these days. What her younger sister was saying made sense. A few days away from Los Angeles, away from this place, did sound appealing, and a change of scenery might help her regain her perspective. Once the urge to cry had passed, Claire took a deep breath and asked, "Exactly which days next week are you talking about?"

"I'm flying to San Francisco on Sunday, the eighth," Ellen told her, "and I've got use of this place until the fourteenth. You'll love it there, Claire, I promise you will. I've got photos of the house and it's positively fantastic! A view that's to die for, and we'll each have our own bedroom and bathroom. We can take day trips into San Francisco, ride the cable cars, go to Fisherman's Wharf, do all those touristy kinds of things. Come on, what do you say?"

Claire picked up her desk calendar. Except for one telephone interview appointment, next week was completely blank. "I'd have to bring some work with me," she said, still hesitant, "maybe spend some time doing phone interviews."

"So what's the problem? Just bring your work along. We'll still have plenty of time to have fun together."

"Well—"

"Do me a favor, Claire, and pamper yourself for once, will you? Trust me, you'll feel a helluva lot better if you give yourself a break. Besides, I really do miss you."

Claire knew that Ellen was right. She was slowly driving herself crazy here at home, with her stomach tied in knots, waiting for the phone to ring or for Charlie to show up at the door again. And, when she wasn't researching or writing something about brutalized and victimized women, she was compulsively scrubbing her apartment's walls and floors, symbolically removing all traces of the husband she was divorcing from her home. Some life that was.

"Okay," Claire said finally. "I guess I can manage to drive up on Sunday afternoon." She would try to finish most of her article on battered women before she left town. Although the fact made her nervous about paying her bills, she had no other firm assignments ahead of her.

"Great!" Ellen said. "Can't wait to see you. Got a piece of paper handy? I'll give you the directions."

Claire wrote down the address of the house in Tiburon as Ellen dictated it to her. "This could be fun," she said, allowing an optimistic tone to creep into her voice for the first time. She put down her pencil and paper-clipped the note she'd just written to her desk calendar.

"Damn right it's going to be fun, Claire. You and I are going to have a good time next week if it kills us."

10

Chewing on her lower lip, Jane stared at the small monogrammed leather suitcase that lay open on the king-size bed. It was empty and she felt no motivation to pack.

"Come on, Janie," Herb said, tossing a third pair of socks into his own suitcase. "Better get going if we're going to be in Big Sur before dark."

"I don't know, Herb. Tell you the truth, I really don't feel much like going away this weekend." She walked over to the window and stared out across the turquoise waters of the bay.

Herb's heart skipped a beat. "But I've got things all set up," he said. "I already paid for the cabin, got us a dinner reservation at Post Ranch Inn for tomorrow night. We need this, sweetheart, we need a romantic weekend away, just the two of us."

"I don't know if it's going to help. I've thought some about marriage counseling, but—"

"I'm not saying we can't go to counseling, too, sweetheart. Anything you say. You got through to me this time loud and clear—you're hurt and you're angry and I can't really blame you. I know I've been spending too much time and money on the galleries lately, that I've been a rotten husband."

Jane turned toward Herb and shot him a skeptical look. "I just don't think I have the energy to keep on trying anymore, Herb. I'm tired."

Herb tried his best to look contrite. "Don't say that, please don't. I—I can't picture life without you." He had nothing to lose by pulling out all the stops now. Hell, he'd get down on his knees and beg if he had to. He couldn't let Jane back out of this weekend trip—his whole plan would crash and burn. There was no way the two of them could still be here on Sunday, when Ellen Merchant showed up for the house exchange. And he couldn't keep Jane from finding out about her missing jewelry and his raids on her bank accounts for much longer, either. Only yesterday, to pay Kozlowski, he'd forged a check that almost cleaned out her personal checking account. Even so, his payment to the bookie was more than seven grand short this week.

Herb crossed the room and placed his hands gently on his wife's shoulders. As he felt her thin bones beneath his fingers, he was reminded of what a small woman she really was—of average height but unusually slim. He outweighed her by a good seventy-five pounds. "I know I've been wrong," he said. "I've neglected you and I'm sorry, but please, Janie, don't punish me by throwing away what we still have together. I'm willing to do whatever it takes to save our marriage, anything at all. Hell, I'll even dress up in a clown suit and help you entertain your hospital kids if you want. Just come away with me, give me this one small chance to start making it up to you." He smiled tentatively. "Promise I'll give you breakfast in bed tomorrow—my famous mushroom omelet and blueberry muffins."

Jane raised her glance and met Herb's clear blue eyes. He looked sincere, she thought, but then he always looked sincere. That was one of her handsome husband's main talents. He could look somebody straight in the eye and swear black was white without blinking. "How about we try counseling first and, if we're making progress, we take a trip together later. Maybe to New York or London, go to the theater, or maybe do that English castle tour we talked about."

He could kill Jane right here if he had to, Herb thought, the benign smile still playing across his lips. He could transport her body down to Big Sur and implement the rest of his plan from there. But that would be much riskier. There might be bloodstains on the carpet if things got messy, or in the Jaguar's trunk. He might inadvertently leave incriminating evidence behind. No, it was much safer to get her down to Big Sur alive and take care of her there. "We'll do it all," he said. "Big Sur now, counseling starting next week, Europe for Christmas if that's what you want." He leaned forward and kissed Jane lightly on the lips, then more firmly. "We're going to make it, sweetheart, I know we are."

"But—" Jane felt her resolve wilting as her body began to respond to her husband's touch. If only she could believe what he was saying. If only she could trust him this time.

Herb crossed the bedroom to his wife's big walk-in closet and threw open the door. "What clothes are you taking, hon? Come on, I'll help you pack."

"You don't need to bother. I'll do it myself." Jane swallowed her doubts and decided to give Herb one last chance. Maybe he really had gotten her message, maybe he was finally ready to grow up. She tossed jeans and sweaters and lingerie into the suitcase, then folded a dinner dress and laid it on top. "As soon as I pack my cosmetics, I'm ready to go," she said a few minutes later.

Herb began to breathe easier, now that it was clear Jane was going to come to Big Sur with him despite her initial reluctance. "I'll go put the food in the car," he told her, carrying his suitcase out of the bedroom.

He loaded his black Samsonite bag, along with an Igloo cooler and two bags of groceries, into the Jaguar while it was still in the garage, then came back inside for Jane's suitcase. When the car's trunk was fully loaded, he opened the garage door and moved the dark green sports car into the circular driveway, where it would be easier for Jane to get in. As he closed the driver's side door and headed back into the house through the front door, Herb noticed Louise Justman peering through her kitchen window, watching him intently. He gave her a curt nod, and her deeply lined face with its thick eyeglasses disappeared behind her curtains.

This time, Herb was not displeased with the old woman's spying on him and his house. He planned to use her nosiness to his own advantage.

A few minutes later, as Herb pulled Jane's car into the street and headed downhill, his mind was focused only on what he had in store for his passenger once they reached the remote cabin he'd rented. He didn't even glance at the vacant lot across the street, where two men were watching from behind some scrub oak trees.

Nor did he notice Sid Balzarian's empty old Chevrolet parked in a turnout half a mile farther down the winding road.

Jane lay across the surprisingly firm queen-size bed in the Big Sur cabin, groggily planning to take an afternoon nap. Now that she was actually here, she thought maybe this weekend retreat wasn't such a useless idea after all. Herb was being amazingly sweet and attentive—he'd insisted she have a glass of wine with the lunch he'd actually prepared himself. Of course, the meal was only a seafood salad he'd bought at a takeout restaurant and packed in the Igloo cooler before they left Tiburon, but he'd washed the dishes afterward, insisting she relax and finish her wine outside on the porch while he labored in the kitchen.

At least Herb seemed to be trying this time, she told herself, and that was a real change from his recent preoccupation and indifference. This cabin he'd found for them was really quite charming, in a primitive sort of way. Set a good half-mile back from the main road and nestled in a grove of pines, it had a small living room with a fireplace, a modern kitchen, and a separate bedroom and bath. Now, with the bedroom window cranked open, Jane could hear nothing but the comforting sounds of a gentle breeze in the treetops and the peaceful twitter of the birds. She began to relax, to feel hopeful about her marriage and her life for the first time in months.

Herb leaned across the bed and gave her a quick peck on the cheek. "Have a good rest, sweetheart. I'm going to take a walk, check out the woods. Be back in an hour or so."

"Careful of the poison oak," Jane warned sleepily. She was feeling the wine she was unaccustomed to drinking so early in the day.

"Don't worry, I know what to look for."

Herb knew exactly what to look for, but it was more than poison oak. He was far more interested in finding out whether there were any nosy neighbors nearby who might thwart his plans. And, of course, he needed to find a secluded spot where he could dig Jane's grave, a place where nobody would ever find her body.

Despite a lingering tingle of guilt that he could even consider killing his wife, never mind actually do it, Herb kept telling himself that this was a matter of sheer self-defense. Unless he got his hands on Jane's money—and there was no way she'd just hand it over to pay his gambling debts—he was going to be dead meat. If he wanted to survive, Jane had to die—it was that simple. So he'd planned everything carefully, using the same analytical skills that helped him choose which teams to bet on and what point margins offered the biggest payoffs. As soon as he'd set up the house exchange with the red-haired Minnesota nurse, he'd found this secluded cabin, using a phony name to rent it for the weekend and paying cash at the rental agency. Nobody would ever think to look for the remains of Jane Parkhurst Carmody here, because nobody would know she was missing, not with her double living in the Tiburon house for the next week, while Herb established the perfect alibi for himself a thousand miles away. Even if, sometime in the future, there was suspicion that Jane had met with foul play, nobody would ever think to look for her here, in the Big Sur woods.

Herb found a path through the trees, carefully circumventing a thick patch of poison oak. He crossed an acre of dense underbrush and took a path downhill through a cypress grove before finding a clearing. Nearby was a dry creek bed, where a stream undoubtedly ran during the rainy winter months. Jane would like this place, he rationalized. She would like her final resting spot to be in the shade of a cypress tree and near a babbling brook. She'd always appreciated nature. He used his walking stick to poke at the soil underneath the thick blanket of pine needles. It seemed loose enough, and not particularly rocky. Certainly digging a grave here would be much easier and less noticeable than trying to clear a spot in that dense underbrush up the hill. Here, he should be able to dig quickly without breaking his back, and this spot was far enough away from the cabin that future weekend vacationers would be unlikely to notice the ground had been disturbed.

With this crucial part of his plan decided, Herb headed back to the cabin. He let himself in the front door as quietly as possible and stole across the living room to the bedroom door, opening it noiselessly. Peering inside the room, he saw Jane still lying on her back on the bed, her eyes shut, her mouth slightly open, and her mop of blazing curls spread across her pillow. The wine at lunch had done its job, he saw, as he fought off a strong urge to cut and run before he had to carry out the next part of his plan. He was on the verge of making his biggest gamble ever—this time he'd put his own life on the line. Yet he couldn't chicken out now. His heart beating rapidly, Herb forced himself to think about Kozlowski and his goons, about what they would do to him if he didn't come up with the cash he owed them, and he reminded himself that Jane was the only feasible source of that cash. No, there was no turning back. He had to see this thing through, and there was no time like the present.

Quietly, he took an extra pillow from the linen closet next to the bathroom and carried it into the bedroom. If Jane awoke before he made his move, Herb would simply say he'd decided to join her in a nap. As he gazed down at her new, still slightly unfamiliar face, he flashed back to the gangly, big-nosed, awkward girl she used to be and a quick rush of compassion almost halted his plan in mid-execution.

Kozlowski, he reminded himself, gripping the pillow until his knuckles whitened. *Kozlowski.* He couldn't forget about Kozlowski. He had to go for broke . . . or die trying.

Herb moved quickly, pressing the pillow down on his wife's freckled face. He felt her jerk awake as soon as the pillow touched her and, for a long, terrible moment, he was afraid she might actually manage to fight him off. Despite her slender figure, Jane was much stronger than he'd anticipated. But he couldn't let her prevail. He threw his full weight on top of the pillow and ignored the thrashing of her arms and legs as she struggled to break free. Soon her movements began to slow and he managed to pin her firmly to the mattress until she lay quiet.

By the time it was over, Herb's pulse was beating faster than it had the time he'd almost won those Olympic swimming trials, and his stomach was churning dangerously. It had probably taken no more than five minutes from the time he'd covered Jane's face with the pillow until he was certain her body was completely motionless, but it seemed more like an hour of hard labor. Cautiously, he lifted the pillow and stared down at his wife. Her eyes were open now, but unseeing, her new face ashen.

Shuddering, he placed the pillow over her face once again, so he wouldn't have to look at her. The enormity of what he'd done suddenly overwhelming him, he spun away from the bed, rushed into the bathroom, and vomited his lunch into the toilet.

When he finally regained his composure, Herb rinsed out his mouth and washed his face. The worst part was over, he told himself as he waited for dusk. When the afternoon's light finally began to dim, he took a shovel from the cabin's tool shed and headed off to the shady spot near the dry creek to dig his wife's grave.

When he awoke the next morning, Herb was so stiff and sore he could hardly move his aching body off the short, uncomfortable sofa—he hadn't been able to make himself sleep in the cabin's only bed, not after Jane had died there.

As he stretched his sore muscles, he had to admit he'd seriously underestimated the difficulty of the task he'd set for himself last night—digging a deep enough grave in soil that turned out to be full of sturdy tree roots, carrying a hundred and twenty pounds through a quarter mile of brush, then burying Jane and obscuring the site so no one could tell it had been disturbed.

Still, he'd done pretty well for a man who'd let himself get a bit flabby, he thought. Maybe the grave wasn't quite as deep as he'd originally envisioned, and he'd stumbled a couple of times as he staggered downhill, Jane's dead weight balanced on his shoulder, but the abundant pine needles around the spot he'd chosen made it relatively easy to obscure the gravesite once he'd managed to bury her body.

Yes, the worst was over. Now all he had to do was cover his tracks. After a long, hot, rejuvenating shower, Herb removed every trace of the Carmodys' stay at the cabin, locked it, and headed north again. At a roadside turnout, he discarded the Igloo cooler and the trash he'd taken from the cabin.

It was Sunday and traffic was light, so he reached San Francisco International Airport half an hour ahead of schedule. After checking both his and Jane's suitcases onto his flight at curbside, he parked the Jaguar in short-term parking.

"I'd like to leave this envelope for Ellen Merchant to pick up," he told the ticket agent at the designated gate. "She's coming in on the flight from Minneapolis-St. Paul." Inside the envelope, Herb had placed Jane's keys and the parking ticket, with the row and space where he'd left the Jaguar noted on the back. He also included a note for Ellen, cautioning her to avoid "our nosy neighbor on the east" and alluding to some vague on-going legal troubles he and Jane were having with her. Might as well head off any inclination the house exchanger might have toward trying to strike up a conversation with old Louise Justman, Herb figured.

"Ms. Merchant know to ask for this here?" the gate agent asked with a quick glance at the envelope.

Herb nodded and watched as the other man slid the slim package under his counter. "Thanks."

As he turned away, Herb checked his watch. He still had an hour before his flight to Seattle was scheduled to leave. Ellen Merchant's flight was due in twenty minutes. He ducked out of the gate agent's view and loitered on the other side of the concourse.

When Ellen's flight arrived, Herb watched nervously as passenger after passenger emerged from the jetway door. He'd bet everything on that single photo in the house exchange book. What if he'd bet wrong?

But he quickly realized he hadn't. Herb knew Ellen Merchant the moment she came through the door. Her eager young face was surrounded by a mass of fiery curls. She was perhaps an inch shorter than Jane, he figured, and dressed in cheaper clothes than Jane would wear, but nobody who didn't know his wife extremely well could tell from a distance that this was a different woman.

He watched as Ellen stopped and asked the gate agent for the envelope, just as she'd agreed to do, accepted it with a quick thank-you, and walked toward the baggage claim area with a big grin on her face.

This one was going to pay off big, Herb told himself as he breathed a big sigh of relief. He'd finally hit the jackpot.

With a long last glance at Ellen Merchant, he picked up his carry-on bag and headed down the concourse to board his flight.

11

The Jaguar handled the winding road leading to the Carmodys' house like nothing Ellen had ever driven. Although she was a bit nervous driving such an expensive vehicle, she really was looking forward to living like a genuinely wealthy woman, if only for a week. Certainly driving a car like this one was part of the package.

As she checked the numbers on the houses she passed, each more elaborate than the one before, Ellen felt like Cinderella arriving at the ball. Finally, there it was. Her breath caught as she saw the street number she was seeking attached to the dramatic gray structure perched on the side of the mountain. The full panorama of San Francisco—the bay, Alcatraz and Angel Islands, and the Golden Gate and Bay Bridges—was visible behind it. She parked the Jaguar in the circular drive and carried her suitcase inside.

Ellen spent the first hour exploring the luxurious house, choosing the master bedroom for herself and designating the guest room, which was almost as elegant, for Claire. Both rooms opened onto a long wooden deck along the back of the house and shared the incredible view. She unpacked her suitcase, hanging her clothes in the closet alongside some of the most elegant designer outfits she'd ever seen, even in *Vogue* or *Harper's Bazaar*. Each of these dresses probably cost a month of her nurse's salary, Ellen realized. Fingering the butter-soft silk on an emerald evening gown, she suddenly felt like a voyeur, like the hired help snooping through the boss's personal belongings. But that was silly, she told herself. For once, she wasn't just working in a fabulous house, she actually *belonged* here. She *lived* here, if only for a week. Yet, she couldn't help wondering what the Carmodys must be thinking of her modest little place in Minnesota. If they were used to this kind of luxury . . .

Ellen took a quick run into town and bought enough groceries for a couple of days, then opened a bottle of wine, poured herself a glass, and relaxed in a redwood rocker on the deck, watching the boats zigzagging across the bay while she waited for Claire to arrive. As she saw the ferry dock at Tiburon and its crowd of passengers disembark, she had a weird feeling she was being watched. She glanced next door and spotted an old woman framed in a side window, clearly staring at her. The litigious neighbor, she thought. The old woman looked harmless enough, but Ellen had worked with enough elderly people to know how irrational they sometimes became. She had no intention of ignoring Herb Carmody's advice to avoid Mrs. Justman. She looked away again.

Ellen had almost finished her glass of wine when the doorbell rang. She threw open the door to find Claire standing there, looking tired and strained, but wonderful. Ellen threw her arms around her sister and hugged her tight. "You look great!" she said, realizing once again just how much she'd missed Claire, the only family she had left.

"So do you, Ellie. And this place! My God, how on earth did you manage this?" Claire set her suitcase and laptop computer inside the door and glanced around, her eyes wide with amazement. "Look at that view!"

"Promised you a palace, didn't I? And we've got a whole week to pamper ourselves in it," Ellen said, grabbing her sister's suitcase and carrying it into the living room. "Hey, I left the garage door open for you. You can park your car inside. Just be careful not the scratch the Jeep."

"But what about that Jaguar? Shouldn't it be in the garage? I don't mind parking mine outside."

Ellen blushed. "It's just that I—I don't think it's a good idea to have your car, uh, visible to the neighbors."

"What are you talking about?"

"Look," Ellen confessed, "I didn't exactly tell the Carmodys I was bringing my sister along, so—"

"You didn't *tell* them?" Claire's jaw dropped. "But I thought—"

"Look, it's no big deal, all right? Mr. Carmody sort of made a point about there only being one of me and, at the time, I didn't know if you could come, anyway. So I—"

"So you let them think you'd be staying here alone."

Ellen nodded. "I guess, basically. Hey, it's not like it's really going to make any difference. I mean, we're not going to hurt anything. They'll never know the difference. Come on, I'll show you your room." She barged down the hall with the suitcase, setting it down in the guest bedroom. "See, Claire, there's an extra bedroom for you, your own bathroom and everything."

"Jeez, Ellie, I feel like some kind of intruder."

"Hey, you'll get over it. Look, Claire, this is an adventure. It probably would have been all right with Mr. Carmody—Herb—if I'd asked about bringing you along. After all, both he and his wife are staying at my place, so fair is fair—two for two."

"But you were afraid if you asked him he'd say no."

Ellen squirmed a bit. She knew Claire was right—she'd gone through the same mental exercise herself half a dozen times. But in the end, she'd elected to be a tiny bit untruthful or, to be more specific, to avoid telling Herb Carmody the complete story. "I guess I *was* a little afraid," she admitted. "Figured, why risk it? Anyway, that's why it'd be best if you just put your car away in the garage. I have permission to drive the Carmodys' Jaguar all week, so we won't even need to take your car out again. Nobody needs to see it."

Taken aback, Claire considered the situation. What were her choices here? She certainly wasn't going to turn around and drive all the way back to Santa Monica, not tonight. She was beat and the prospect of going back into Charlie country so quickly was distinctly unappealing. Once she'd talked herself into taking this vacation, she realized how much she really needed it. She looked around at the house. This place, with its pale silk upholstered furniture and lush ivory carpeting, its grand piano, and most of all, its billion-dollar view, was like a fantastic luxury hotel. This was a vacation spot she'd never be able to afford under any other circumstances. "So am I going to have to hide out all week?" she asked.

Ellen shook her head. "Luckily, the Carmodys have some kind of legal feud going on with the old lady on the east side, and she's the only one who seems to have a clear view of this place. Apparently they don't even speak to each other, so there's nothing to worry about there. Just put your car out of sight in case somebody the Carmodys know drives past and wonders what it's doing here. I mean, why should we go looking for trouble?"

"Seems to be your motto lately," Claire scolded.

"Come on, don't pull the big sister act on me. We're going to have *fun* this week, Claire, unless you've completely forgotten how. Go on," she said, making a shooing motion with her hands. "Go park your car in the garage and I'll pour you a glass of wine."

As soon as he checked into his hotel in Seattle, Herb went down to the dark oak-paneled bar and struck up a conversation with the bartender while nursing a Bud Lite. They discussed the baseball season, specifically whether the Mariners had a chance to win the World Series this year. "Betting on either the Giants or the A's myself," Herb offered. "Gotta stick with my home teams." Avoiding a second drink—ever since that drunken evening when Sid had driven him home, he'd been very careful to watch how much alcohol he consumed—he charged the bill to his room and added an overly generous tip.

"Thank you sir," the bartender said, noticing the tip.

"Hey, you don't have to 'sir' me. Name's Herb Carmody. Just a working stiff like you, Josh," he said, reading the bartender's name off his badge. "In town for the week to meet with some of the local marine artists."

"You an artist, Mr. Carmody?"

"Herb. Wish I were, but I don't have that kind of talent. Sure do appreciate it, though. I'm an art dealer myself. Got me a couple of marine art galleries in the San Francisco area."

The two men chatted for a few more minutes before Herb made his way into the dining room, where he made a similar point of introducing himself to the waiter and over-tipping. By the time he went upstairs to his room, he felt certain these people would remember him. And throughout the week, the artists with whom he had appointments would be able to vouch for his whereabouts as well.

Before he crawled into the king-size bed, Herb performed one last task on the mental alibi list he'd put together. He called FTD and ordered a dozen yellow roses to be delivered to Jane at his house tomorrow. "I want the card to read, 'With all my love,' no signature," he instructed. "She'll know who they're from."

Good work, he congratulated himself, as he hung up the phone. Surely that flower delivery truck would draw Louise Justman's attention. If she hadn't already, the nosy old bitch would see the red-haired woman at the house receiving the flowers and draw exactly the conclusion he wanted her to draw.

As he crawled into bed, Herb finally began to feel his anxiety fall away. The nightmare of killing Jane, then burying her in the woods, seemed long ago now, not merely last night. Here he was, already a thousand miles away, his alibi firmly established. He could feel this, the biggest bet of his life, beginning to pay off just the way he'd planned it would.

By the time the week was over, he would return to Tiburon ready to play the part of the surprised husband whose wife has apparently left him despite his demonstrated devotion to her . . . or maybe he'd be simply the husband whose wife has gone to take care of her ailing mother or on a trip to Europe. He could decide that sort of detail later. In her absence, he would siphon off Jane's assets, several thousand bucks at a time, until Kozlowski was fully repaid and Herb was as free as the lone seagull in that painting he'd hung in the window at Waves. Then his old luck would be back for good.

Eventually, he figured as he lay in bed staring at the ceiling, he might risk having Jane declared dead so he could inherit her entire fortune, but that would be years from now. How long did it take before you could have someone who disappeared declared legally dead—five years? Ten? He didn't know. For now, he decided as he pulled the blanket up to his neck and turned onto his side, he'd have to be careful not to appear too greedy. Greediness would only attract attention. No, in the next few weeks and months, he would do nothing more than get himself out of debt and take enough extra cash to enjoy himself during Jane's "extended vacation."

His bones aching with the physical exertions of the past twenty-four hours and his thoughts dancing amongst the possibilities for a bright future free of threats from either

Kozlowski or his wife, Herb fell into a deep sleep.

By eight o'clock the next morning, Claire had begun setting up her home office on a table she'd pushed against one wall of the Carmodys' restaurant-size kitchen. She was an early riser by habit and had already eaten a quick, light breakfast by the time Ellen emerged from the master bedroom.

"You're not actually going to work on our first day here, are you?" Ellen said as she came into the kitchen, rubbing the sleep out of her eyes. She grabbed the coffee pot and poured herself a cup.

"Just until lunchtime. Then we can go sightseeing if you like," Claire replied. "I warned you I had to finish my story for *Glamour* this week." She unplugged the kitchen telephone, plugged a small black box with a wire protruding from it into the phone's wall jack, then reconnected the telephone.

"What's that thing?"

"Hooks up to my tape recorder so I can record my phone interviews, make sure I get the quotes right."

"I thought that was illegal," Ellen said, frowning. "Isn't that how that woman from the President's impeachment trial got into all that trouble?"

"Linda Tripp. No, recording a call isn't illegal, as long as both parties know it's being recorded. Where Tripp screwed up is by not telling Monica Lewinsky she was recording their calls."

"Right, like Monica would have said, 'Sure, go ahead, tape all my darkest secrets, I'm into that.'"

"Which, of course, is exactly why Tripp didn't ask her. But luckily I'm not trying to entrap anybody. I always ask my interview subject's permission before I turn on the tape recorder, then I ask again and get the agreement on the tape. Don't worry, I'm not going to jail for wiretapping." Claire set up her laptop on the table and spread out her notes for her battering story, along with a few photos she'd taken of the women she'd interviewed at the battered women's shelters.

"My God," Ellen said, grabbing one of the photos and staring at it in horror, "what happened to her?"

"Boyfriend took a knife to her face. Didn't like other men looking at her, so he made sure they'd never want to again."

Ellen shuddered, dropping the photo back onto the table. "Sometimes I don't know how you can stand to write about this stuff, Claire, honest I don't."

"Come on, Ellie. You must have seen far worse than this when you worked in the hospital."

Ellen thought for a moment. "Sure I did, but somehow it seemed different. I was trying to *help* people who got hurt, not—" She caught herself in mid-sentence.

"Exploit them?"

Ellen blushed. "Well, sort of," she admitted. "Sometimes it does seem like that's what you're doing."

Claire furrowed her brow. *Was* she exploiting her subjects? "People certainly don't have to talk to me," she said in defense of her work. "And I'm not writing about this stuff to titillate anybody. I want to help my readers understand the causes of violence and show them how to recognize the signs it might be heading their way. Besides, a lot of people I interview find it validating, even therapeutic, to tell their stories to somebody who actually *listens* to them."

Ellen took a long sip of her coffee and rubbed her left eye. "Why don't you just admit it, Claire? You're still trying to understand why Mama used to beat you up when she got drunk."

And would have beaten you, too, if I hadn't stopped her, if I hadn't taken your blows for you, Claire thought. But that was a subject she never discussed with her younger sister.

She'd decided years ago that Ellen didn't need to know— she'd only end up feeling guilty, and that wouldn't change anything. Instead Claire said, "Hey, I've already been in therapy once, Dr. Freud." That had been years ago, when she'd first moved to L.A. Therapy was "in" in L.A. "I'm perfectly aware of what I'm doing," she added, "but my personal motivation has nothing to do with whether what I write is valuable to my readers."

"Point taken." Ellen grabbed a slice of bread and popped it into the fancy combination toaster and convection oven. "So how about we take the ferry to San Francisco this afternoon, walk around the waterfront for a while and pick up dinner at a Chinese restaurant?"

"Great, as long as I get this one last interview finished by the time we have to leave." After drafting most of her article, Claire had realized she needed to add a few quotes from a female police officer who'd worked with battered women.

Ellen held up her palms in a peace-making gesture. "Okay, okay, I promise to leave you alone and let you work." She quickly spread peanut butter on her toast, put it on a china plate, and carried it into the dining room.

After she'd showered, Ellen found she still had time on her hands. Claire was working in the kitchen—she'd finished her phone interview and was now using her computer to transcribe her tape. If only she hadn't finished her mystery paperback on the plane, Ellen thought. It might be fun to sit out on the deck and read for a while. Maybe she should drive into town to buy a morning newspaper, yet it seemed a long way to go for a fifty-cent purchase. And, by the time she got back, Claire might be finished working and there wouldn't even be time to read the newspaper.

Ellen's gaze fell once again on the open closet and the elegant clothes hanging inside. She could see that Mrs.

Carmody had wonderful taste—each and every outfit was in precisely the color Ellen would have chosen for herself, assuming she were rich enough. There were electric blue and emerald green silks, russet and chocolate wools, even a teal cashmere sweater and skirt. She rummaged through the dresses, noticing that many had small labels sewn inside that read, "Handmade for Jane Carmody." Talk about class! The woman actually had her own private seamstress.

Ellen took a royal blue silk taffeta strapless ball gown off its hanger and held it up against her body in front of the full-length mirror. The brilliant color made her hair seem even redder in contrast, and the dress appeared to be just about her size. What the hell, she thought impulsively. She climbed out of her jeans and T-shirt and stepped into the dress. The fabric felt a bit stiff against her skin and the skirt bunched slightly on the floor, but if she wore a pair of extra high heels, she felt she could attend any snooty party San Francisco had to offer and fit right in with the highest of high society.

She pinned her hair on top of her head and preened in front of the mirror, admiring herself from every viewpoint. She knew she shouldn't be touching Mrs. Carmody's clothes, of course, but surely the woman would never find out. Ellen felt like a child again, playing dress-up in her grandmother's attic. She felt magical.

She rummaged in a dresser drawer to see if she could find some costume jewelry to complete the image. A necklace and matching earrings of rhinestones or pearls and perhaps imitation sapphires would be perfect with this dress. She found no jewelry—probably a woman as rich as Mrs. Carmody wouldn't be caught dead with the kind that could be tossed into a dresser drawer, Ellen concluded—but she came upon a stack of photographs apparently taken at some sort of society party. She leafed through them, stopping abruptly as she came upon a shot that might almost have been of her. A smiling young woman with bright red hair posed next to a handsome blond man. Amazingly, the redhead was wearing this very dress, with a necklace and earrings not much different than the ones Ellen had envisioned. Except, in this case, she felt sure they weren't costume jewelry at all, but the real thing, obviously worth thousands of dollars. Seeing the photo left her with a strange, eerie feeling.

The doorbell rang. Startled, Ellen dropped the photos on the dresser top and froze, her sense of fun instantly converted into naked guilt.

"Claire, can you get that?" she called toward the kitchen. "I'm not dressed."

She prayed it wasn't one of the Carmodys' friends at the door. She'd be caught two different ways—Claire wasn't supposed to be staying here, and Ellen had no business trying on Mrs. Carmody's dress. Frantically, she tugged at the zipper at the back of the bodice, but it was stuck. She couldn't budge it. *Damn!*

She breathed a small sigh of relief when she finally heard the front door slam shut. She tried the zipper for what seemed the dozenth time, but still couldn't manage it. Feeling like a thief caught with her hand in the till, she crept contritely into the kitchen to find Claire placing an arrangement of yellow roses on the gleaming granite countertop.

"Where'd those come from?" Ellen asked.

Claire spun around. "They're for Jane Carm—" Her jaw dropped as she saw her sister. "What on earth are you doing in that getup?"

"Don't yell at me, please, Claire. I know I shouldn't have tried on the dress, but I didn't think it would hurt anything." Ellen stared at the floor like a chastised child. "The zipper's stuck," she said in a small voice. "Can you help me out of this thing?"

"Jeez, I sure hope you've learned your lesson," Claire said as she worked the zipper free of the fabric caught in it. But she was secretly glad Ellen couldn't see her face—she was having trouble stifling a laugh over her sister's obvious embarrassment.

"I know, I know. I won't touch anything else in that closet, honest," Ellen promised.

With the zipper finally unzipped, Ellen clutched the bodice of the dress against her bare breasts and began to back out of the room. She noticed the roses again; they were the long-stemmed kind. "You said somebody sent those to Jane Carmody?"

Claire picked up the card. "Right. I think the woman's got a lover. Look at this," she said. "It's signed, 'With all my love,' and there's no signature. I thought Jane Carmody was supposed to be in Minnesota with her husband."

Ellen raised an eyebrow and smirked. "She is. They're staying at my house, but apparently her boyfriend doesn't know that. Hey, maybe I don't feel quite so bad about trying on her dress anymore, not if she's that kind of woman."

The two sisters giggled conspiratorially. "If Lady Jane is fooling around with somebody, she's probably lucky these flowers will be dead and thrown away before she and her husband get back here, right?" Claire said. "So we might as well enjoy them." As an afterthought, she admitted, "I still don't approve, but you really do look smashing in that dress." Ellen had always been the prettier sister. Claire knew that, even if Ellen hadn't been born with that eye-catching head of red hair while her own was plain, ordinary brown, people would have noticed her first.

"Maybe I'll meet some rich prince this week and end up being able to afford clothes like this myself," Ellen said dreamily. "Even a house like this."

"Right. And maybe Spielberg will buy the movie rights to my *Glamour* article and I can buy the mansion next door to yours. Now go and change back into your jeans. I finished my interview and I'm ready to see San Francisco."

"Want to see something really weird first?" Ellen asked. Claire nodded.

"Come with me." She led the way back into the master bedroom and handed Claire the photograph of the red-haired woman and her male companion.

"It's the same dress," Claire observed, "and—and, geez, she sure looks a lot like you!"

"Got to be Jane Carmody, right? Its label said the frock had been made specially for her."

Claire stared at the photo. "This is really amazing. Jane Carmody could be your double, if you don't look too close."

"Which is probably why her clothes are so perfect for me. Think that's her boyfriend?"

Claire considered the photograph. "Uh uh," she said. "He looks much too uncomfortable in that monkey suit to be that woman's boyfriend. I think this is the husband."

"Herb, the guy I arranged the house exchange with."

"Right. Besides, Lady Jane wouldn't leave a photo of lover boy lying around, would she?"

As Ellen stepped out of the dress and put her jeans and T-shirt back on, she turned to Claire and asked, "Hey, you don't suppose Jane Carmody is trying on *my* clothes, do you?"

Claire shot her a withering look. "Not unless either she or Herb has a nurse fetish," she said. "Go get your purse. Let's go catch the ferry."

"There she goes," Sid Balzarian said to Barry O'Farrell. "Can't miss that hair."

"Or that Jag," Barry agreed, reaching for the keys that dangled from the van's ignition. He stopped in mid-reach. "Shit! She ain't alone. What's with the other broad? We sure as hell ain't gonna snatch two of 'em."

After a mid-morning drive past the Carmody house, where they'd seen the green Jaguar parked in the circular drive, the two men were watching the street from the front seat of a van Barry'd borrowed from his brother-in-law's plumbing business. They were parked half a block downhill from the Carmody house. In this ritzy neighborhood, they figured, nobody would wonder about a plumbing vehicle parked for hours on the street; somebody was always remodeling a bathroom or a kitchen or putting in a hot tub. The downside was that they'd been sitting in the van for the past three hours as its interior heated up in the sun and the atmosphere inside was getting riper and riper. Even with the windows rolled down, it was horribly hot, yet they dared not run the air conditioning. A parked plumbing truck might not be noticed, but a parked plumbing truck with its motor idling all morning would surely draw attention.

"So we try again tomorrow," Sid said, wishing Barry had used a better deodorant. "Maybe Mrs. Carmody'll be alone then."

"Why don't we just come back and snatch her tonight?"

"That ain't gonna fly. Use your brains, Barry. We already agreed we can't risk grabbing her at the house—who knows what kinda security system they got? Besides, Herb's gonna be home at night, and he can't know nothing about this scam 'til it's time to collect the dough."

"Shit, Sid, don't know if I can get the van tomorrow. Denny was pissed enough about me taking it today. Hadda tell 'im my own piece of shit broke down, I hadda get to a job interview in Oakland."

Sid thought for a moment as he watched the Jaguar snake

down the hill. "You can't get the van tomorrow, maybe I can borrow my ma's old Caddie. It's got plenty of trunk space. We can throw the broad in there." However they did it, he figured, they couldn't drive their own vehicles.

Barry shook his head. "Jesus fucking Christ, man, you're gonna try to pull off a kidnapping in a rust-bucket seventy-nine Caddie? Lucky if you can even get that old piece of crap started."

For the next five minutes, they argued about the relative merits of whatever vehicles they might be able to borrow from friends or relatives, resolving nothing.

Sid sighed, beginning to wonder whether bringing Barry in on this deal was the brightest move he'd ever made. "So try telling Denny the job wants you back for a second interview," he suggested. "That don't work, we'll rent us something from U-Haul."

Barry made a rude sound. "U-Haul in *this* neighborhood? Talk about sticking out like a sore thumb. Jesus! Okay, okay, I'll talk to Denny. That don't work, I'll get my sister to lean on him. She really tries, she can talk that horny old bastard into anything. Way she keeps naggin' me to get a job, I figure it's time she did a little something to help out."

"Hey," Sid said as the larger man started the van, pulled away from the curb and cranked the air conditioning up to high, "you gotta remember this is our chance to make it big, man. That red-headed bitch is worth almost half a million fucking bucks to each of us." Hell, he'd been thinking, if they could get away without letting Herb Carmody know they were the ones who'd taken his wife, maybe they wouldn't have to give him a dime. Of course, he wasn't about to share that brainstorm with Barry, not yet, anyway.

By the time they reached the bottom of the hill, the Jaguar was nowhere in sight, but that didn't really matter, Sid figured.

They had to pick up the Carmody broad when she was alone, and when the chance of anybody witnessing the snatch was minimal. When she was parking her car on her way to the ferry or leaving the beauty shop, something like that. He had no doubt they'd eventually find the right time and place, as long as Barry didn't get so impatient he fucked up the whole deal.

"Screw this," Barry said, wiping his brow despite the struggling air conditioner. "I've had it for today. Where the hell can I get me a Big Mac?"

By Wednesday morning, Ellen and Claire had fallen into a routine—in the mornings, Claire worked on her article at her kitchen-table office while Ellen sat out on the deck, reading one of the new paperback books she'd bought in San Francisco. In the afternoons, they went sightseeing together. They'd spent Monday and Tuesday afternoons exploring San Francisco—doing touristy things like taking a trolley ride from North Beach to Union Square, having a glass of wine in the bar at the top of the Bank of America Building and marveling at the view, exploring Chinatown's tiny, crowded streets and shops, and hiking the waterfront trail, starting at the San Francisco Yacht Club and going across the old Presidio grounds as far as the base of the Golden Gate Bridge.

On Wednesday afternoon, the sisters planned to stay on their side of the bay and drive to Muir Woods to see the giant sequoia trees, some of which Ellen's guide book claimed had grown to be 250 feet tall. But by mid-morning, the fog had rolled in, followed by a light drizzle.

"You still game to hike through the woods in this weather?" Ellen asked when Claire took a short break from her computer.

Claire looked outside. The fantastic view had disappeared; now all she could see through the glass wall facing

San Francisco was the water-soaked deck and fog, endless fog. "Maybe it will burn off by this afternoon," she suggested.

"Maybe." Ellen was bored. Half the fun of spending her mornings reading was that she could enjoy the view and the sunny weather, but today there was no view and she couldn't even sit outdoors. It was almost like being back in Minnesota on a rainy day. "Tell you what," she said. "We're almost out of bread and I ate the last of the fruit. I'll drive down to the grocery store, pick up a few things, and then maybe poke around the souvenir shops for a while. If the weather doesn't clear up by lunchtime, we could go to a movie this afternoon and have dinner at home."

"Whatever," Claire replied, absent-mindedly. She was already back at her computer, her thoughts lost in figuring out how best to work into her *Glamour* article the advice of one of the psychologists she'd consulted. "Drive carefully," she murmured as her sister grabbed her windbreaker and headed out the front door.

"Bingo," Barry said as the Jaguar passed the parked plumbing van. "The bitch is finally alone."

"Don't let her get too far ahead," Sid warned as Barry started up the van and U-turned to head downhill. "She makes it onto Tiburon Boulevard, no way we're gonna know which way she's gone."

"I know how to drive," Barry snapped. By his third day in his brother-in-law's van with only Sid's company to pass the time, his irritation was showing. "Chloroform?"

Sid pulled out a small brown bottle of liquid he'd ordered over the Internet and a large rag from underneath the passenger seat. "Don't worry. She ain't gonna be able to ID us. Sneak up behind her, dose her with this stuff, and she won't know what hit her."

They followed the Jaguar onto Tiburon Boulevard and drove slowly past as they saw the luxury car enter the parking lot of the town's only supermarket.

"Wait 'til she goes inside, then grab that spot right next to where she's parked," Sid said, craning his neck to watch what the redhead was doing. "Wedge in there, between her and that blue Mercedes."

Barry followed orders.

Fifteen minutes later, they saw the woman they'd followed emerge from the market carrying two sacks of groceries, her handbag dangling from her shoulder and her fiery hair dampened and frizzed by the incessant drizzle.

Ellen carried her purchases to the Jaguar and set down one of the plastic bags on the damp pavement while she fumbled in her purse for the car keys. She opened the trunk and put her purse inside for a moment as she arranged her groceries. But before she could reclaim her purse, straighten up, and close the trunk, she felt strong fingers grip her shoulder. As she attempted to spin around and protest the unexpected assault, a rough cloth was clamped tightly across her face. Instantly, she became aware of a strong, chemical odor and her keys dropped to the pavement, skidding away out of reach. She fought vainly for breath as her vision went blurry and her muscles turned to jelly. Quickly, everything faded to black and she slumped toward the pavement.

With Sid standing guard at the open rear doors of the van, Barry caught the now-unconscious woman under her arms and dragged her, heels scraping, across the six feet of pavement to the back of the van. Sid helped him load her into the space they'd cleared amongst the pipes and hoses and plumbing tools. Barry climbed in after her as Sid closed the van's doors from public view.

Barry bound the drugged woman's limp hands and feet with a length of plumbing tape, then blindfolded her with a greasy rag while Sid slammed shut the loaded trunk of the Jaguar and headed back to the van, his eyes nervously surveying the parking lot for any observers. There were few people in the lot at this hour, however, and none of them seemed the least bit interested in anything but completing their own errands before being soaked by the drizzle.

Barry climbed through the back of the van and into the driver's seat, then started the vehicle and shoved into gear. "She's still knocked out good," he reported, a smile of victory beginning to creep onto his lips. He glanced at the dashboard clock. "Less than three minutes since we grabbed her. Not bad for a couple fucking amateurs, eh?"

"Not bad at all, pal. You tie her up good and tight?"

"Used that plastic plumbing tape, just like you said. Stuff's made to stop a sewage leak—she sure as hell ain't gonna bust outta that."

"And the blindfold?"

"Stop worryin' about every fucking little thing, willya, Sid? We—"

"No names!" Sid hissed. "I told you that!"

"Okay, okay, I forgot." Barry glanced over his shoulder. "She's still out like a light, didn't hear nothing."

"Just drive us to the house and we'll carry her up to the room before she's awake enough to give us a fight. By the time we call Herb tonight and get the bucks arranged, she'll have slept it off and be ready to cooperate."

In the back of the van, Ellen lay unconscious, her hog-tied and blindfolded body buffeted back and forth against the plumbing equipment as the van turned and bumped its way north.

12

"Hey, look what I found!" Stuart Draeger said as he sauntered across the supermarket parking lot after cutting out of school during lunch hour. He swooped down, using his index finger to hook a set of car keys off the pavement.

"Somebody dropped their keys. Big fucking deal." His buddy Jason Pringle wasn't impressed with Stuart's find, but then Jason wasn't impressed with much of anything these days, the sole exception being Linda Anderson, the girl with the biggest tits in their tenth grade class. Linda, predictably, didn't know the pimply-faced fifteen-year-old was alive.

"These aren't just keys, dick-head. These are *Jaguar* keys. Ever driven a Jag?"

Stuart already knew the answer to his question; he'd asked it only to put Jason down—his friend's phony been-there-done-that attitude was getting old fast. He knew Jason had never driven anything, at least not legally. Stuart, on the other hand, was already sixteen and had his learner's permit. He'd driven his mom's Lexus a dozen times, and his dad had promised to let him drive his Mercedes as soon as he had more experience behind the wheel. His dad had even promised him a new BMW for high school graduation if he got into his alma mater, Stanford, but that was looking pretty doubtful. To make the grades he'd need to get into Stanford, even as a legacy and with his dad's fat alumni contributions, Stuart knew he'd have to quit the weed and study a whole lot harder. He wasn't sure it was worth it. Even if he ended up at San Francisco State, his dad would have to buy him wheels, and he'd much rather have a bitchin' SUV with oversized tires than a yuppie Beemer, anyway. Still, the Jaguar parked next to the keys he'd found was way cool.

After a quick look around the parking lot to see if the car's owner was anywhere in sight, Stuart pushed one of the keys into the driver's side door. It clicked and turned easily. He pulled the door open, slid onto the lush black leather driver's seat, and adjusted it to fit his long legs.

"What the fuck you doing?" Jason demanded.

"Come on. Get in, quick, before somebody sees us!"

Jason hesitated for a few seconds, shifting his backpack from one shoulder to the other. "You fucking nuts? We could go to jail, Stu."

"You forget, limp dick—my dad's a lawyer. Come on, let's see how this baby handles on the road."

Jason lurched to the other side of the car and climbed into the passenger seat. He'd barely managed to close the door before Stuart peeled out of the parking lot and headed north on Tiburon Boulevard.

Lost in her work, Claire continued to ignore the rumbling of her stomach and stare at her computer screen. She highlighted a sentence, then shifted it to a higher spot in the paragraph. There, she decided, that read much better. Another morning's work on the writing, and maybe another follow-up call or two to double-check some quotes, and her article would be ready to send off to *Glamour*. She saved what she'd written, backed it up on a diskette, shut down her computer, and felt strong hunger pangs once more.

She glanced at the oak-rimmed clock on the kitchen wall. It was just after one o'clock. How long could Ellen spend wandering around those tacky souvenir shops near the ferry pier, anyway? Claire was quickly becoming annoyed with her younger sister's tardiness.

She glanced out the living room window. The fog still hung over the bay, but it was beginning to dissipate. Now she could see the faint outline of the San Francisco skyline across the bay, looking like an Impressionist painting. The drizzle seemed to have stopped. They could probably hike Muir Woods this afternoon after all, assuming Ellen got her butt back here within the next few minutes. Otherwise, they'd run into commuter traffic on 101.

Increasingly irritated, Claire foraged through the refrigerator, which was about as big as the coat closet in her Santa Monica apartment. She managed to find only an opened jar of peanut butter and a few pieces of stale bread. She toasted a slice of bread, spread it with the peanut butter, and ate it standing up, looking out the kitchen window at the street for any sign of the Jaguar. If Ellen brought something tasty back from the store, Claire decided, she'd nibble on that as well. It was hours since she'd had that leftover muffin for breakfast and she was still hungry.

When two o'clock arrived and Ellen still hadn't returned, Claire's annoyance began to turn to worry. Her sister might be half an hour, even as much as an hour late, but now she should have been back at least two hours ago. Claire began to visualize Ellen involved in a terrible traffic accident and realized she didn't even know the license number of the car her sister was driving. Maybe she should call the police and ask if there'd been any accidents involving a dark green Jaguar. How many cars fitting that description could there be around here? On second thought, there were probably plenty of Jaguars around here, Jaguars of every possible color, along with every other make of expensive, ostentatious car. Marin County was status car country.

Should she take her own car and drive through town looking for Ellen? Maybe she'd find her, assuming she'd gone no farther than the village of Tiburon. But what if she left the house and, while she was gone, Ellen was trying to call her here? Claire cursed herself for not having a cell phone like all her friends. It was this damn freelance work she did—the money she earned came in so sporadically that she dared not commit herself to paying even one more monthly bill.

By three o'clock, Claire had decided to risk looking foolish. She phoned the Tiburon police.

"No traffic accidents reported in town so far today, ma'am," a polite woman officer told her.

"No car-jackings or anything like that?" Claire asked, another hideous thought creeping into her mind. Certainly that Jaguar was the sort of car a car-jacker might covet.

"Nothing reported. If your sister's still missing tomorrow, give us another call, okay? We'll see about filing a missing person's report. But I'm sure she'll be back by then. Probably just ran into a friend or decided to go shopping. We see it all the time."

Claire insisted upon leaving her phone number in case any disaster involving Ellen Merchant was reported later today, but she hung up without feeling much confidence that the cop had taken it down.

This couldn't be Charlie's doing, could it? What if her soon-to-be ex-husband had somehow found out where Claire was staying and had decided to throw a scare into her by way-laying Ellen? No, surely that was ridiculous. *Wasn't it?* She'd checked the messages on her home answering machine just a few hours ago, hoping one of the editors she'd submitted article ideas to had called to offer an assignment. But there were only two calls, both from Charlie, sounding pissed off as usual.

Still, Charlie wasn't the sort to follow her all the way up here and then take out his rage on Ellen. *Was he?* Claire tried to put the thought out of her mind. If Ellen wasn't back shortly, she could always call Charlie, she told herself, at least see if he answered the phone at his new apartment or was on duty at the restaurant.

By four o'clock, Claire decided she'd waited in the house long enough. She took her own car out of the garage and drove down the hill, then around the circle of downtown Tiburon, past the supermarket, the library, the real estate offices, and the ferry station. She passed the souvenir shops slowly, not really believing that Ellen could still be inside one of them, inspecting a stack of Tiburon T-shirts or some gaudy china figurines. She looped through each of the town's parking lots, but there was no sign of either Ellen or the green Jaguar.

Feeling frightened and defeated, Claire headed back up the hill to the Carmody house.

She felt a strong pang of disappointment as she rounded the final bend and saw that the Jaguar was not in the driveway. She'd almost convinced herself that Ellen would be waiting at the house with some wild, irresponsible tale to explain her absence. But the house was dark, it's gray rough-cut siding damp and gloomy-looking in the foggy afternoon light.

She parked her car in the garage next to the Jeep, closed the overhead door, and went back inside the house.

Shortly after six o'clock, the phone rang with a startling blast. Claire nearly jumped out of her skin as she leapt to answer it.

"Ellen?"

"Put Herb Carmody on," a muffled male voice demanded.

Claire felt deflated again. "Sorry, Mr. Carmody's out of town this week," she explained. "May I take a message for him?"

There was a long pause on the other end of the line.

"Hello? Do you want me to take a message for Mr. Carmody?" she repeated.

"Who are you?"

"Claire Merchant, the house sitter," Claire improvised. "Who're you?"

"Don't matter who *I* am. Where's Carmody?"

Claire bristled at the caller's demanding tone. "I told you, he's out of town. If you don't want to leave a message, you can call him back on Sunday."

Another pause. "*Fuck!* Listen, lady, you get hold of Carmody fast, tell him to get his ass back here. We got his wife. He wants to see her alive again, he's gonna get us a million bucks by Friday. And no cops or she's dead. We'll call back, tell him how to deliver. And you keep your mouth shut to anybody but Carmody, got it?"

Claire was so stunned she could think of nothing to say.

"Got it?"

"But I don't—"

"Find Carmody and tell him." The line went dead.

Claire sank down into the chair facing her computer. This didn't make any sense. Herb Carmody and his wife Jane were at Ellen's place in Minnesota—weren't they? So how could somebody have kidnapped Jane and expect Herb to be here?

Ellen! With a terrible feeling of dread, Claire recalled the photograph of Jane Carmody that Ellen had found in the dresser drawer and her own remark that Jane could be Ellen's double. Frantic, she ran into the bedroom, found the photo, carried it back into the kitchen and stared at it under the bright overhead light. The two women were hardly twins, but a strong resemblance was definitely there, in their slender builds and, of course, their stunning red hair. That's the main thing someone who didn't know either of them well would notice, Claire realized, the hair. It made sense that anyone who saw a red-haired woman driving Jane Carmody's car would undoubtedly think he was looking at—that he was kidnapping—Jane Carmody.

Claire grabbed the phone and dialed Ellen's number in Minnesota from memory. She would call the Carmodys and they would work this thing out, somehow, before Ellen got hurt. *She had to believe that.*

But the phone rang and rang. On the eighth ring, Ellen's phone machine picked up. Claire didn't leave a message. The house exchangers must be out, she figured. She prayed they'd be home soon.

During the next hour, Claire dialed Ellen's home number five more times with the same result. It was eight o'clock here, but already ten in Minnesota. Restaurants in the Midwest closed much earlier than in California. If the Carmodys had gone out to dinner, surely they would be back at Ellen's place soon. Unless . . .

A neighbor, Claire thought. She could call one of Ellen's neighbors and make sure the Carmodys had arrived according to plan. Ellen had often mentioned one particular woman in the neighborhood she considered a friend. Lillian, Gillian, Marian . . . no, Vivian, that was it. Vivian something. Claire searched her mind but drew a complete blank on the neighbor's last name.

She hurried back into the master bedroom and searched through her sister's luggage until she found a small address book, then leafed through the pages until she found Vivian Henderson listed, with an address in the same block as Ellen's. It would be nearly eleven o'clock there now, but this was a true emergency. Claire dialed the number.

"Hello," a sleepy female voice answered.

"Vivian? Vivian Henderson?"

"Who is this? Lord, you know what time it is?"

"I'm sorry, Vivian. This is Claire Merchant, Ellen's sister. Something's happened and—"

"What—is Ellen all right?"

"I think—I hope so—but I need to ask you a really important favor. Do you know if the Carmodys are still using Ellen's house? I have to get hold of them right away and nobody answers the phone over there."

"Can't say as I've seen anybody around. Hang on a minute. Let me see if they've got any lights on." A moment later, Vivian came back on the line. "House is dark as a tomb," she reported.

"Oh, dear," Claire said. "I'm not sure what to do. It's really urgent that I contact them right away."

"Told Ellen she was a damn fool to let complete strangers use her house." Vivian Henderson sounded even more annoyed.

Claire couldn't argue her point, not under the circumstances. Yet it seemed irrelevant at the moment; there was no going backward. "Is there anything else you can suggest?" she asked. "It really is urgent that I reach them. A—a major family emergency." She didn't bother to explain that the emergency was in Claire's family, not the Carmodys'.

"I've got a key to Ellen's house," Vivian announced. "She's got one to mine, too, just in case. You never know, a person could fall down the stairs and break her neck, or be raped and murdered in her bed or—well, you know." She sighed loudly. "I s'pose I could get dressed and go over there."

Vivian Henderson sure was a ray of sunshine, Claire thought ironically. That image of Ellen being raped and murdered in her bed certainly helped alleviate the anxiety she was already feeling. But all she said was, "Oh, thank you, Vivian.

Would you? I'm really sorry to have to ask. I know it's late, but—"

"Yeah, I know, it's really, really important."

Claire heard the other woman sigh again, then a rustling, probably of bedclothes.

"Give me your phone number there," Vivian said. "I'll go check and call you back."

When the phone rang ten minutes later, Claire picked up on the first ring.

"No sign anybody's been there," Vivian reported. "No suitcases, nothing. Appears nobody's used the bed or the bath towels or the dishwasher, and Ellen's plants haven't been watered. Looks like you got a couple of no-shows on your hands."

"Thanks, Vivian," Claire said.

"Want me to call the police or something?"

"No, I don't see what they could do. If the Carmodys do show up, though, will you call me again?"

"Sure enough, first thing."

Claire hung up the phone with shaky hands, a feeling of complete helplessness overwhelming her. After all those years when she'd managed to protect her little sister from Mama's battering fists, she'd thought her work in that area was over. But now, when they'd both managed to make it to adulthood, Ellen was being threatened again, by a new, even more potent evil.

Claire would manage to save her sister this time, too, somehow. There was no doubt in her mind about that. As ever, there simply wasn't anybody else to do it.

Still, she had no easy answer to the big question—how?

When Ellen awoke, she was lying on something soft, unable to move her hands and feet. She couldn't see, either, and it felt as though something rough was tied around her eyes. What was happening to her? Had she had some sort of massive stroke? She had no memory of anything since carrying her groceries out to the car. As her grogginess began to lift, she gradually became aware of the combined odors of mildew and oil. Her muscles were cramped and stiff and she tried to move her limbs, but something seemed to be holding them uncomfortably in place. She moaned in pain and frustration.

"Hey, she's waking up," a deep male voice said.

"'Bout time," a second man with a higher voice answered. "Don't worry, Jane, nobody's planning to hurt you."

Was he talking to her? "I—I'm not—I'm not Jane," Ellen mumbled sleepily. At least she could still hear and she could still talk.

"Yeah, and Willie Brown ain't mayor of San Francisco. Don't bullshit us, lady. We know who you are."

"I can't move," Ellen complained. "My arms and legs hurt and I can't move them." Was this simply a vivid nightmare? If so, she didn't seem able to wake herself.

"Ain't gonna move, 'less you cooperate real nice. Then maybe we think about untying you."

The fog enveloping Ellen's mind slowly evaporated and she stiffened against her bonds. "Cooperate *how?*" She could hear the fear in her own voice. Were these men planning to rape her? Or maybe they already had, while she was unconscious. Her body felt battered and bruised enough. Perhaps they planned to sell her into white slavery. Did white slavery even exist anymore? Of course it did, in concept anyway, but it was probably called something more politically correct nowadays. Her skin crawled as she thought about what else could happen to her, helpless as she'd been rendered.

"We called your house," the second man told her. "This broad answers the phone and says your husband's outta

131

town, but she's gonna find him. Soon's we get our million bucks, we let you go."

"*What?* I don't have any husband and I don't have any million dollars. You must have me mixed—"

Ellen felt sharp fingers grab her already-aching shoulder and shake her violently. "*Told you not to bullshit us!* We been following you for the past two weeks, lady—we know you're Jane Parkhurst Carmody, Herb Carmody's wife. We know your old man, Parkhurst, made a fucking fortune importing liquor and he left it all to his little girl—none other'n you. Shit, you ain't even gonna miss a lousy mil, all the fucking dough you got. But, hey, Jane, it's your choice—you wanna be cheap, go ahead—it's your life."

Ellen tried hard to think this through. Her mind was still fuzzy from whatever they'd used to drug her, but she was beginning to comprehend the mess she was in. Whoever these two baboons were, they obviously believed she was Jane Carmody and they were demanding a million-dollar ransom from her husband to set her free. If only she could convince them they had the wrong woman, surely they'd let her—

Ellen stopped herself in mid-thought. But *would* they let her go if they realized they had the wrong woman? Maybe not. Jane Carmody had money, probably a huge fortune, while Ellen Merchant had nothing but a half interest in an old house in Minnesota. She probably couldn't put together a *thousand* dollars in a hurry, never mind a *million*. Assuming these guys were actually prepared to kill Jane if her husband didn't pay the ransom, why wouldn't they kill Ellen as well, if only to make sure she didn't go to the police and ruin their chances of kidnapping the real Jane when she returned from Minnesota?

Ellen quickly realized she was better off letting her kidnappers think she was Jane, not simply a red-haired house exchanger who happened to be driving Jane's car. As long as they believed she was Jane, there was a better chance they'd keep her alive—at least until they found out no money was going to be handed over. The subterfuge would buy her time to figure out how to escape or to wait for help to arrive.

"Okay, okay, you're right," Ellen said, as though they'd managed to convince her of something important. "I'm sure Herb will get you the money, just as soon as my sis— Just as soon as he gets back. Now, please, can somebody untie me?" She tried a ploy she'd seen in a dozen crime movies—"I've got to use the bathroom, really bad,"—and was surprised to find it was actually true.

"Figured you'd see it our way," the second man said. "Gonna untie you, but you gotta keep that blindfold on 'til we tell you. You take so much as a peek at us, we're gonna havta ice you. Got it?"

"I understand."

Ellen was yanked into a sitting position. She felt cold, sharp metal scrape against the tender skin of her inner wrists and flinched. There was a faint sawing sound and suddenly her arms were free. She swung them around to the front and flexed her sore muscles. The same process was quickly repeated on her ankles.

"Gonna leave now, lock you in," the man told her. "Keep that blindfold on 'til we tell you from outside the door or we havta kill you."

"What about the bathroom?" Ellen asked, worried. "I really do need a bathroom."

"Got a private one attached to this room," the man said with a mean laugh. "Figured we hadda have plush accommodations, a rich bitch like you checking in to our little hotel."

Ellen heard a door slam, followed by the sounds of a key being turned in a lock and one of the men calling out that she could remove her blindfold now. She pulled it off and realized it was the source of the greasy odor. Repulsed, she flung it away.

She saw she was in a square room, perhaps twelve feet on a side, obviously meant to be a bedroom. She was lying on an old maroon couch shoved against one wall. There was a scarred oak hardback chair, the kind she used at her kitchen table in Minnesota, in the far corner, and a floor lamp standing at the edge of the worn gray sculptured carpeting. Otherwise, the room was devoid of furnishings.

On one wall was an empty closet and on another a window, boarded up from the outside. A third wall held both the sofa on which she was sitting and the door from which the men obviously had exited. The fourth wall had another door, standing ajar. Ellen soon discovered it led to an old-fashioned bathroom with a chipped pedestal sink, an iron-stained toilet, and a cast iron bathtub with claw feet. Everything in the place was filthy. Still, she lowered herself onto the toilet seat, grateful for the small pleasures of having her limbs unbound and being able to relieve herself without her kidnappers watching.

When she'd finished, Ellen grabbed one of the two grimy-looking towels hanging from the towel rack and, using the half-bar of soap in the tub's soap dish, did her best to clean up both herself and the bathroom. She was too well trained a nurse not to appreciate the value of sanitary surroundings. If she was going to be staying in this miserable cage until somebody—Herb or Claire or the police—freed her, or she managed to escape, at least she didn't have to live in filth.

Claire's glance fell on the small tape recorder sitting next to her laptop computer on the kitchen table. *Damn!* Why hadn't she thought of switching it on when the kidnapper called? The device she'd used to record her last magazine article interview was still connected to the telephone's wall jack. If only she'd remembered to hit the record button, at least she'd have gotten the kidnapper's voice on tape. She wouldn't make that mistake again, she decided—next time the phone rang, she'd switch on the recorder before answering it.

She made sure that all the connections were tight, but knew that was a minor effort in the battle to find and save Ellen. Her first move had to be to find the Carmodys, to let them know what was going on. She dared not call the police—the kidnappers might be watching her, or maybe they even had a mole in the police department. She couldn't chance that. She would have to heed the kidnappers' warning not to go to the cops.

Certainly there had to be a clue somewhere in this house that would tell her where the Carmodys had gone, Claire thought. Obviously, they'd had some last-minute change in plans. Think, she ordered herself. *Think!* What had Ellen told her about these people?

Mainly that they were rich as sin and lived in a gorgeous house in Tiburon, she recalled. And that was the source of all this trouble, not its solution. Where did their money come from? Claire wracked her brain to remember if Ellen had told her anything pertinent. Art, that was it. Herb Carmody was some sort of art dealer. Maybe he dealt in rare paintings worth hundreds of thousands of dollars. Was it possible that commissions from auctioning rare art could make him wealthy enough to live like this? Yet the art in this house didn't run to Renoirs or Rembrandts. It was a collection of pleasant enough seascapes and paintings of clipper ships, probably worth thousands, but not hundreds of thousands of dollars.

The San Francisco area was full of art galleries, Claire knew. She grabbed the Yellow Pages and found several dozen listed, none of which would still be open at this late hour. There was nothing called the Carmody gallery, but she wasn't even sure that Herb actually had a gallery. For all she knew, he could be a broker working out of an office somewhere.

She decided the only thing she could do now was search the house methodically. Surely she'd find something helpful—maybe a phone number for a close relative who might know where Herb and Jane could be reached, or at least the name of Herb's business. It seemed so odd that they'd just go off like that, leaving a total stranger living in their house, without so much as leaving behind a phone number where they could be reached in case of emergency.

Claire found nothing useful in the kitchen. All she uncovered there was a stash of family recipes and some old grocery lists and a drawer holding a stack of receipts from a local grocery store that offered home delivery. If you were this rich, she guessed, you didn't even have to bother with doing your own marketing; the market came to you.

Claire hoped the master bedroom would be more promising. She went through each inch of the tall chest of drawers methodically, no longer feeling the least bit guilty as she plowed through Herb Carmody's underwear and socks and his stacks of carefully folded white shirts. After all, her sister had been kidnapped because of these people!

The triple dresser was obviously Jane's, and Claire was momentarily impressed as she fingered the woman's handmade lingerie. Each pair of panties and slip was pure silk—no comparison to her own nylon and cotton—with a tiny personal label sewn inside. Like that evening gown Ellen had tried on, these items were labeled, "Handmade for Jane

Carmody." Talk about self-indulgence. How many homeless kids could have had a decent dinner, or how much cash could have helped fund one of the battered women's shelters Claire'd visited if Jane had donated the difference between what the things in these drawers had cost and the price of equivalent items at Macy's?

Claire slammed shut the last of the drawers and began searching the closets. On the top shelf of Jane's closet, hidden behind a stack of straw sun hats, she found a gray metal box with its key still in the lock. She pulled it down, set it on the bed, and opened it. It was full of papers. Perhaps there was a clue here to who the Carmodys were. Claire glanced at each document in turn. There was a photocopy of the deed to this house, in Jane Carmody's name alone—title was held as the "separate property of Jane Carmody, a married woman."

Interesting, Claire thought, wondering what the significance might be. Beneath the deed, neatly typed on a Santa Barbara brokerage house's stationery, was a list of stocks and bonds with a total worth of nearly fifteen million dollars. The box also contained some old check registers and four bank books for certificates of deposit that were about to mature, worth a total of more than three hundred thousand dollars. Another statement was for a money market account with a balance of more than eight hundred thousand. Every one of these documents, like the house deed, was in Jane's name alone.

No wonder somebody thought kidnapping Jane Carmody would be a way to rip off a quick million dollars, Claire thought. The woman was loaded. And this was just her own money. It was possible her husband had his own separate assets as well, that the Carmodys were one of those modern couples who kept their finances completely separate from each other's. Claire wondered briefly if she'd have been better off doing that with Charlie. Probably not, she decided. Charlie had turned into a pain in the butt, but she had to admit he'd always earned more than she did.

Claire picked up the last of the papers in the metal box, copies of Jane's birth certificate and her father's death certificate. But before she could add them to the pile on the bed, she saw what lay at the bottom of the box—a small, almost feminine revolver with a carved pearl handle—and her breath caught. She'd always been repulsed by guns, although there'd been a time early in her marriage when she'd given into Charlie's request that she accompany him to the shooting range. Much as she hated the deafening noise and the overpowering stench of gunpowder, she'd turned out to have a naturally accurate aim. Years later, she realized her good eye was precisely why Charlie's interest in guns had faded so quickly—he didn't like his wife beating him at anything, certainly not the manly sport of target shooting. For her own part, Claire was delighted never to have to hold another gun and, writing the kind of articles she had lately, stories centered on violence against women and children, had only strengthened her feelings of revulsion.

She picked up the revolver and saw that it was fully loaded. Quickly, she shoved it back into the metal box and stuffed the papers back on top of it. She'd learned some things here, she realized—that Jane was rich beyond her own imagination, and that she didn't mingle her wealth with her husband's, if he had any. She also learned that the woman who owned this house felt the need to keep a loaded gun.

But, unfortunately, nothing she'd found so far gave Claire a clue about where the Carmodys were right now, or how to get that information. She put the box back on the closet shelf and replaced the hats in front of it.

Her search of the guest room produced nothing of interest, nor did her examination of the living room and dining rooms. How odd, Claire thought. Surely these people must pay bills, and they must have tax records and receipts. Where did they keep them?

Perhaps in one of the linen closets in the hallway, she thought. She pulled open the first hallway door and found nothing inside but stacked sheets and towels, all of them expensive and many of them monogrammed JPC.

Feeling more and more frustrated and frightened for Ellen, Claire pulled open the second door. But this was no linen closet. This door opened onto a stairway leading to a lower level of the house. Of course! She suddenly felt incredibly stupid. The house was built into a hillside, and houses of this type almost always had more than one level. Why hadn't she thought of that sooner?

Claire found the lower level of the structure to be much smaller than the upper, with just enough space for two rooms and a bath between them. One room was used as an office and the other a den, with black leather furniture and a big screen TV dominating one wall. Claire noticed there was also a locked gun cabinet in the den, displaying a selection of rifles and shotguns behind its glass doors. So the husband was into guns, too.

She decided to attack the office first, and it was here that she hit pay dirt. Clipped together in the top desk drawer was a sheaf of bills addressed to Jane Carmody, all of them for a patient named Adeline Parkhurst at a nursing home in Santa Barbara. From the paperwork she'd found upstairs, Claire realized that Adeline Parkhurst was Jane's mother. She wondered whether Jane might have told Mrs. Parkhurst where she was going this week. Yet, if the old woman was ill enough to live in a nursing home, Claire didn't want to alarm her unless there was no other recourse.

She leafed through the other bills, all of them for amounts

that would put her into bankruptcy if she had to pay them, and then moved onto the file cabinet.

In the lower drawer, she located the Carmodys' joint tax returns for the past seven years. She pulled out the one for the most recent year and examined it. Jane's income was entirely from interest, dividends, and capital gains—clearly she didn't have a paying job. But Herb listed himself as owner of two small businesses, Waves and Waves II, identified on the tax returns as art galleries.

Claire grabbed a phone book off the desktop and found phone numbers for both businesses. As she might have expected at this late hour, phone machines answered both numbers, but recorded messages cited the hours during which Waves and Waves II would be open for business tomorrow. She decided against leaving a message of her own; there was nothing to be gained from alarming Herb's employees. She'd simply call again as soon as the galleries opened in the morning. Surely, Herb Carmody must have told his employees where he could be reached.

Claire felt the adrenaline rush that had given her the stamina to search this entire house evaporate, and a wave of exhaustion crashed over her. She climbed back up the stairs like an arthritic old woman carrying an extra hundred pounds on her back.

She had to get some sleep, she realized, if she was going to be any help at all to Ellen tomorrow. She sank onto the bed in the guest bedroom but, despite her physical exhaustion, sleep was slow in coming.

Every time Claire closed her eyes, she was assaulted with another vivid image of the terror Ellen must be feeling. It was hours later before she fell into a fitful sleep.

Herb left his hotel room and headed for the concierge's desk. He'd had a successful day, having arranged for a dozen marine art works to be shipped to his Tiburon and San Francisco galleries and sold there on consignment. Even more important, there were now three Seattle artists who could vouch that he'd spent the entire day here in the Northwest. Now he figured he'd earned a little relaxation.

"Where's the nearest sports bar?" he asked.

The concierge lowered his voice. "Looking for a little action?"

Herb nodded. "Don't mind placing a small wager or two, just to pass the time."

"Try Champion's." The concierge gave Herb the address. "They have a good clientele there, a lot of fulltime sports buffs, and the cops leave the place alone," he said. "Should I call you a cab?"

Herb shook his head. "Thanks, but that's not necessary," he said. He plopped a ten-dollar bill on the concierge's desktop. "Appreciate the advice."

An hour later, he was seated at Champion's bar with fifty bucks riding on the outcome of a college track meet. It wasn't a large enough bet to get him really excited, but until he got back to Tiburon and began to access Jane's income, he was hamstrung by the daily limit of three hundred in cash that he could pull out of the hotel's ATM machine.

While he was in Seattle, Herb had given a lot more thought to how he would play Jane's disappearance after he returned to Tiburon. He'd decided the best way was to tell people she'd left him a note saying she was taking an extended vacation in Europe. That would explain her Jaguar's being left at SFO. He could intimate that his wife was visiting doctors overseas, maybe seeking a cure for some rare disease, or having more plastic surgery, assuming anybody asked about her. Of course, he'd act as baffled as anybody else when she didn't return as scheduled. Could she have met foul play? Decided to stay on? Met another man and fallen in love? Any of those scenarios might work, but he didn't have to decide that yet. Time was on his side now.

In the meantime, however, Jane's fat interest and dividend checks would keep arriving in the mail and Herb would deposit them into their joint checking account, from which he could withdraw funds at will. In no time, he'd have Kozlowski paid off, his galleries back in the black, and plenty of money left over for new bets. With Jane's money to wager and multiply, he'd soon have more than enough dough to set himself up the way he'd dreamed, ever since he was a poverty-stricken boy.

Reassuring himself that his luck had finally turned for the better, Herb glanced up at the television set just in time to see his pick in the five thousand meters stumble and fall in the pack as it rounded the final turn of the track. Some tipster that Stoli drinker at the end of the bar had turned out to be!

"Damn it to hell!" Herb pounded his fist on the bar in a sudden flash of anger, bumping his beer and slopping some of the suds over the side of his thick glass mug.

The bartender shot him a warning glance as he wiped the bar top clean.

Oh, well, Herb quickly consoled himself. He'd only lost a lousy fifty bucks, and his bet on this race had been nothing more than an impulsive guess at best. It wasn't like he'd bet on one of *his* teams, the Giants or the 49ers or America's Olympic swimmers. If he lost a bet on a sport and a team he actually knew something about, then maybe he'd have to take it as a sign.

But no way was he going to interpret this tiny setback as notice that his string of bad luck wasn't yet completely dead and buried.

It was—it had to be! Right along with Jane Parkhurst Carmody.

13

At precisely nine thirty the next morning, Claire dialed the first number she'd copied from the phone book.

"Waves," a female voice answered on the fifth ring. The woman sounded out of breath, as though she'd just run into the store from the parking lot.

"May I speak with the manager, please?" Claire asked.

"I'm the manager, Marlene LeBaron. What can I help you with?"

"Herb Carmody owns this gallery, right?"

"Right, but he's out of town this week. I'm sure I can help you."

Claire took a deep breath. "Actually, it's nothing to do with the gallery," she said. "I need to talk to Mr. Carmody right away. Do you have a phone number where he can be reached?"

"What's this about?"

This wasn't going to be as easy as she'd hoped, Claire realized. She would have to explain. "My name is Claire Merchant," she said. "My sister Ellen and I are staying at the Carmodys' house and there's been a—there's been an emergency situation I need to reach them about. They were supposed to be at Ellen's house in Minnesota, but they never arrived and—"

"*Minnesota?* I don't understand."

"They arranged a vacation house exchange with my sister. But, like I said, the Carmodys never showed up at Ellen's place—I had a neighbor check to be sure—and I really do need to reach them right away."

"A house exchange! How odd. Herb completely pooh-poohed the whole concept when I mentioned it a few weeks ago. Actually, my husband and I are going on a wonderful house exchange vacation to Paris next—"

"I'm sure you'll have a great time," Claire interrupted, feeling increasingly impatient, "but right now I have to reach Herb—Mr. Carmody. He must have had a last-minute change of plans, and I thought you'd know where to reach him. It's very, very important."

"Well, of course I know where he is—he'd never leave town without telling me how to contact him. But this Minnesota vacation thing just doesn't sound right. Herb's in Seattle on business—he's had this trip planned for at least a couple of weeks—and I never heard a word about Jane's going along. Plus he *certainly* never said anything to me about going to Minnesota."

Claire caught the derision in the woman's voice, as though no one in their right mind would go to Minnesota on vacation or for any other reason, and she bristled. "Look, Marlene, all I'm asking for is the phone number where I can contact Mr. Carmody," she said. "This is an *emergency*." Why was the damned woman being so stubborn?

"What sort of emergency?" Marlene was sounding more and more suspicious. "There hasn't been a fire or a broken pipe or something, has there?"

"No, no, nothing like that," Claire said. "It—it's rather personal. Please, just tell me how to reach the Carmodys."

"What did you say your name was?"

"Claire Merchant," Claire repeated, beginning to drum her fingertips on her kitchen table desk. "Mr. Carmody made the arrangements with my sister, Ellen Merchant." Exhausted with the strain of the past day, she had all she could do not to lose her temper. Obviously Marlene knew how to reach Herb and Jane. Why in hell wouldn't she simply give her that information? Instead, she was treating her like a stalker or someone who might be mentally deranged.

"Tell you what, Claire," Marlene said, finally. "I don't think it's a good idea for me to give out the name of the hotel where Herb's staying, or the phone number there. I'll contact him myself. If there's anything to this house exchange business, I'm sure he'll call home as soon as he can. That should take care of it, right?" She sounded doubtful.

Claire sighed. "As long as you call him right away and let him know it's urgent that I speak with him. *Absolutely urgent.*"

"I'll call up there as soon as we hang up, but I can't guarantee I'll be able to reach Herb. I know he's got a lot of appointments this week. He may already be out for the day."

"Just *try*, please, right away. It could be a matter of—" Claire stopped herself. She knew nothing about Marlene LeBaron; if she let anything slip about her sister's having been kidnapped by people who'd mistaken her for Jane, it might cost Ellen her life. Or, if Marlene didn't believe her, she'd be even more convinced Claire was a nutcase. "Just do your best," she said, finally.

"I always do my best," Marlene snapped. "Like I said, I'll ask Herb to call home as soon as I reach him."

Consumed by equal feelings of anger, hope and dread, Claire hung up and sat at the kitchen table staring at the phone, waiting for it to ring.

Ellen tried for the hundredth time to lift the window in the room where she'd been confined, but it wouldn't budge. Either it had been nailed shut or the many coats of paint on its frame had sealed it for eternity. She could see a slim crack of daylight through the boards nailed to the outside of the window, just enough to show her it was a sunny day out. Yet any hope that she could somehow escape this room was quickly fading.

Maybe this horror was her punishment for wanting to be wealthy, Ellen thought, or for trying on Jane Carmody's clothes and searching through her private things. She knew she shouldn't have done those things, but her snooping had seemed such a minor infraction at the time. Did this punishment really fit her crime? Still, she felt she had to admit, if only to herself, that she was at least partially responsible for this nightmare. If she hadn't been driving Jane's car, reveling in the childish fantasy that she was Jane or could become Jane, if only for a week . . .

Ellen had slept poorly, with both fear and self-recrimination coursing through her mind. She'd huddled on the moldy old sofa, trying not to breathe in its rancid smell. Although she'd used her raincoat as a blanket, she was constantly cold during the night and, by morning, she was famished as well. She'd eaten only one piece of toast and a cup of coffee in the past twenty-four hours.

Just when she'd begun to wonder whether her captors intended to let her starve to death in this room, there was a knock at the door.

"Hey, Mrs. Carmody, you awake in there?" one of the men called through the door.

"Yes, I'm awake," Ellen replied.

"Thought you might be getting hungry, so we brung you some food. Go in the bathroom and close the door," he ordered. "Try sneaking a look at us when we take in your tray, you ain't gonna live to eat. Got it?"

"I understand," Ellen said. She did exactly as she was told. As she waited inside the bathroom for the man to tell her she could come out and eat whatever food he'd brought, she noticed there was no way to lock the bathroom door from the inside. If the time came when she felt the need to protect herself from these men, this small room would provide her no safe haven.

"Wait'll you hear the bedroom door slam shut. Then you can come out," the man called.

When Ellen emerged from the bathroom, she found a plastic tray holding a dry-looking American cheese sandwich on white bread, a sealed package of corn chips, and a can of Coca-Cola perched on the sofa. She seldom ate what her nutrition courses classified as junk food, but she was hungry enough now to down every morsel of this unhealthy repast.

When her stomach was full, Ellen found her dark mood beginning to lift. She reassured herself that it was an excellent sign that her kidnappers had fed her, however poorly, that it was another good sign they kept worrying about her seeing their faces and being able to identify them. Obviously, the two men were planning to keep her alive and let her go as soon as . . .

Her mood quickly nose-dived as she finished her thought—*as soon as they get their million-dollar ransom.* She knew full well, of course, that no ransom money would be forthcoming. And then what would the kidnappers do with her, Ellen Merchant, a nurse with no noticeable financial assets, a woman who'd had the misfortune to be mistaken for Jane Carmody?

Her strange breakfast began to flip-flop in her stomach.

Herb had just finished shaving when the phone in his hotel room rang. He grabbed it on the second ring and immediately recognized Marlene's voice on the other end. "Hey, how's business?" he asked her. After a good night's sleep, he'd managed to repress his chagrin over last night's bad bet and was in a pretty good mood.

"Slow, as usual," Marlene reported. "But that's not why I called. Had a really weird phone call this morning, and I promised I'd contact you right away."

Herb sank onto the bed, immediately anxious. Surely Jane's body couldn't have been found—he'd buried her well enough, hadn't he? Nor would Kozlowski try harassing his galleries' employees about his gambling debts—the man had nothing to gain from that. "What about?" he asked warily.

"Woman named Claire Merchant called the gallery. Claims she's staying at your house, she and her sister. Something about you're supposed to be on a house exchange vacation—to Minnesota of all places. Is that right?"

Momentarily, Herb could think of nothing to say and his mind raced frantically. Who the hell was Claire Merchant? He'd arranged the house exchange with a woman named Ellen, the redhead who looked so much like Jane. And the last thing he wanted Marlene to know was that Jane wasn't at the house this week. If Marlene found out about Ellen, his alibi would tank in a flash!

"Herb, you still there?"

"Yeah, sure. Just trying to figure out what this is all about."

"So you didn't arrange for any house exchange in Minnesota?" Marlene asked.

"Hell, no," Herb lied. "Why would I do something like that?" His pulse was racing almost as fast as his mind. "What else did this woman tell you?" He was almost afraid to hear the answer.

"That there was some kind of emergency at your house. But she was very secretive, refused to tell me what the problem was."

"How bizarre! I have no idea why somebody would make up a story like that." Herb did his best to sound confused instead of nearly paralyzed with fright.

"Me either, but it certainly is a strange coincidence, isn't it? Here, I was telling you all about how Nick and I are going to do a house exchange vacation in Paris, and now this Claire woman calls the gallery and claims—"

"Must be some friend of Jane's," Herb said, "that's all I can think. Could be Jane's got some oddball houseguest staying with her while I'm out of town, maybe one of those strange theater people she hangs out with. Probably playing some kind of prank. I'll call home, see if Jane knows what this is about."

"So she's not up in Seattle with you, then?"

"Jane? Of course not. You know how she hates these business trips. Not a damn thing for her to do but wait in the hotel for me to finish meeting with my artists. She stayed home, as usual. By the way, I got some gorgeous new pieces on consignment, including a really spectacular sculpture of a blue whale and her pup." Perhaps if he changed the subject, Herb hoped, Marlene would forget about that house exchange business.

"Hope they sell faster than what we've already got," Marlene said. "We're running out of storage space in this place. Say, why don't I just call Jane from here? No need for you to make a long distance call at those rip-off hotel rates."

Herb stiffened, his panic increasing. "No, no, don't bother, really," he insisted. "Hey, it's Wednesday, right? Now that I think about it, Jane always goes to her health club on Wednesday mornings, for her massage. You just worry about the gallery, Marlene. I'll take care of this little prank or misunderstanding or whatever it is myself."

"Hey, you're the boss. Just wanted to let you know I'm always happy to help out."

"You're a treasure, Marlene, don't think I don't appreciate that. Can't think how I'm going to manage when you're off in Paris for two weeks." Herb struggled to make his tone light, although he felt like someone had just dropped a hundred-pound boulder on his chest.

"Back to work, then," Marlene said. "Let me know what you find out, okay?"

"Sure thing, and thanks for letting me know."

Herb hung up the phone, took a deep breath, and dialed his home number with a feeling of utter dread.

Claire sat by the phone in the kitchen, drinking her fifth cup of black coffee. She was already fidgety from so much caffeine, but she couldn't think of anything else to do except wait for the phone to ring. She prayed that Herb Carmody's employee would find him fast, before the kidnappers called a second time and she had to figure a way to stall them.

It was ten-thirty when the phone finally rang. Claire punched the record button on her tape recorder just in case, then picked up the receiver with a trembling hand. "Carmody residence."

"This is Herb, Herb Carmody," a tentative male voice said. "Is this Ellen?"

"Thank God your assistant found you!" Claire said, relieved. "This is Ellen's sister, Claire. I've been staying at the house with Ellen. Tried to call you at her place in Minnesota, but—"

"Uh, sorry about that. Jane and I had a last minute change of plans. Her mother got sick and she had to go to see her, and my Minnesota business plans fizzled. Didn't want to disappoint Ellen, so I rescheduled some business here in Seattle and—"

"That's not important now. At least I finally found you!" Claire related the story of her sister's kidnapping as concisely as she could, trying not to sound as panicky as she felt. "These people obviously think Ellen's your wife, and that you'll pay a million dollars to get her back," she concluded. Despite her best efforts, she was breathless and shaking all over by the time she'd finished her tale.

"But who?" Herb asked. "Who would do such a thing?"

"How would I know?" Claire retorted. "Obviously, it has to be people who know you or your wife, who know you've got lots of money. Which, by the way, neither my sister nor I do. I've been absolutely frantic. I didn't know what to do, whether I should call the police, or—"

"*No!*" Herb shouted into the phone. "No. Whatever you do, don't call the police. Not—not when these people threatened to kill your sister if you do. Think about it—they might be watching you. They could find out. Let me think a minute." There was a long pause. "I—I guess the best thing is for me to get the next flight home. We can figure out what to do after I get there."

"What about your wife?"

"I'll get in touch with her, warn her to stay away. If these crooks are watching the house, the last thing we need is for Jane to come back home."

"I've been thinking the same thing."

"Don't worry," Herb said. "We're going to work this out. Just stay in the house in case they call again. If they do, tell them I'll be home by tonight, and that I can't start getting the ransom money together before tomorrow, at the earliest. That should hold them off for a while."

"They said we had until Friday."

"Plenty of time," Herb said. "Just stay there by the phone. And, whatever you do, *don't* call the police."

In Big Sur, Lester Klemp was on his daily outing with his

dog, Pete, hiking through his fields, shotgun in hand. As usual, Pete darted well ahead of Lester, sniffing the bushes, plunging through thickets of poison oak with impunity, and chasing every bird or rodent he saw. The dog was completely invigorated by his daily breath of freedom.

Also as usual, Lester stopped to survey his cash crop, the marijuana plants hidden from the DEA's snooping helicopters by the feathery overhanging branches of a cypress grove. The tender plants were undisturbed, he noted. They'd soon be ready for harvesting and would bring in enough cash to get him through another winter in his Big Sur cabin. With luck, he might be able to afford that new transmission he needed for his old Chevy pickup as well.

As Lester reached the end of the cypress grove and headed down toward the dry creek bed, Pete doubled back and approached his owner, barking fiercely.

"What's up, old boy?" Lester asked.

Pete began to whimper, obviously disturbed by something.

Alarmed by his dog's unusual behavior, Lester fingered the trigger on his shotgun. "What'd you find, Pete?" He envisioned walking into an encounter with DEA agents searching his fields on foot instead of from their usual helicopter, and briefly considered heading back home. But that would accomplish little. If they'd found his plants, they'd simply check the county property records, discover who owned this little piece of paradise, and arrest him tomorrow or the day after. Might as well follow Pete and find out what was disturbing him now as wait for trouble to descend on him later. "Show me, boy, come on, show me what you got."

Pete led Lester along the dry creek bed. As they reached the edge of a grove of trees, the dog began to growl.

"What is it, Pete?"

Pete dropped to his belly and crawled toward a spot beneath the trees where the ground had obviously been disturbed. Pine needles had been scraped away by marauding animals, and Lester noticed something with a coppery tint mingled in with the freshly disturbed dirt.

"Come on, boy, let's take us a look."

What Lester found was the last thing he expected. The body of a young woman, buried in a shallow grave, had been partially uncovered and ravaged by animals. The odor of decaying flesh hung in the air, despite the morning's breeze. The coppery color, Lester quickly realized, belonged to the dead woman's long, curly hair. He felt sick.

What should he do? Calling the sheriff up here was out of the question. The woman obviously had been murdered—she sure didn't bury herself here—and a murder investigation would bring a cavalcade of county deputies onto Lester's land, maybe even the FBI. Their presence was the last thing he needed, especially now, right before his crop was ready for harvest.

"Come on, Pete," Lester said, backing away while pulling on the dog's collar. "Let's get back to the house, do us some thinking on this thing."

Ellen felt she might go crazy, confined to this dark, dreary room. She'd spent half an hour trying to scrape the crusted paint away from the window frame, using the aluminum flip-top from her can of Coke, but she'd made little headway and eventually her makeshift tool broke in her fingers.

As the sun shifted westward, she peeked through the crack in the boards again and found herself looking directly at a bird's nest. That surely meant she wasn't being kept on the first floor. *Damn!* Even if she managed to open this window and pry away the boards, she might well be injured or killed trying to jump a full story or more onto the ground. She tossed aside what was left of her flip-top paint scraper.

There had to be some way out of here, there simply had to be. If only she knew more about what was going on. Who were these men? Had they called Herb Carmody's house? If so, had they talked to Claire? They obviously still thought she was Jane, so if they'd reached Claire, at least her sister had been smart enough not to tell them the truth.

Ellen pressed her ear to the hallway door. She could hear the faint rumble of voices, but couldn't make out any words. The men were probably downstairs, she figured. But maybe there was another way to eavesdrop on their conversation. She pulled at a corner of the worn carpeting until she managed to work it loose, then folded back the wedge along with its pad. She wrinkled her nose in disgust as she breathed in what had to be years of accumulated dust. Underneath the padding was plywood sub-flooring. She bent down and pressed her ear against it. The men's voices were a bit clearer now.

" . . . oughta be back . . ." Ellen thought she heard one of them say.

" . . . again . . . show on the road," the other replied.

Then the voices stopped. Either the men had stopped talking or they'd moved out of the room below hers.

Once again, Ellen found herself trapped without diversion in this silent, dark and lonely prison. She stood up and stretched her aching muscles, then pushed the triangle of carpeting back into place.

"Lemme talk to Herb."

Claire instantly recognized the kidnapper's voice from his earlier call. Luckily, this time she'd rewound the tape after talking to Herb and switched on her tape recorder again before answering the phone. "Herb's not back from out of town yet," she explained. "I only just reached him, but he's taking the first flight he can get. If it's on time, he should be home by tonight."

"You clue him in about the, uh, situation we got?"

"Of course. He said to tell you he'd start getting the money together as soon as he gets back . . . as long as you don't hurt his wife. I'm sure he's going to want to talk to her, though, make sure she's okay, before he hands over a million dollars."

"He gets home, starts getting our money ready, we put her on the phone."

Claire felt a little better. Ellen was still alive, however frightened or even injured she might be. "I'll tell Mr. Carmody," she replied.

"We'll be in touch," the man said. The line went dead.

At least she'd stalled off the kidnappers for a while longer, Claire thought. What would happen next was the real issue. There was no doubt that the Carmodys had the money the kidnappers were demanding. A million dollars wouldn't even dent the fortune represented by that list of stocks and those certificates of deposit she'd seen hidden in the metal box on Jane's closet shelf.

But whether these rich people would be willing to spend a dime of their wealth to ransom Ellen was another question, one Claire simply couldn't answer. And, until she knew what Herb had in mind, there wasn't much more she could do. Still, he'd been adamant that she shouldn't call the police. That was a good sign, wasn't it? If he intended to shrug this off as not his problem, he wouldn't care whether she called the cops or not.

Claire hung on to that shred of hope for the rest of the day. It was all she had.

Herb pushed his way down the jetway and onto the Alaska

Airlines 727, his carry-on bag slung over his shoulder. He shoved aside someone else's garment bag and wedged his own smaller bag into the overhead compartment, then dropped into the aisle seat and fastened his seat belt. Luckily, no one took the seat beside his. At least he'd have a little privacy during the flight.

Herb had avoided thinking too much about the predicament he found himself in since talking with Ellen Merchant's sister. There'd be close to three hours on the plane for that task, he'd kept telling himself. That would give him enough time to figure out how to handle this unexpected turn of events.

But now the time to consider his options had arrived, and he was forced to admit his run of bad luck wasn't over after all. Or maybe it wasn't that complicated—he just hadn't realized where his change of luck would be coming from, so he'd stupidly acted too quickly. Patience had never been Herb's long suit.

If only he hadn't killed Jane last weekend, he told himself, feeling more foolish now than guilt-ridden over the actual act. If he'd never seen the Merchant woman's photograph and cooked up this ill-fated house exchange idea, he'd have stayed home in Tiburon. Tight-fisted Jane would have been kidnapped, and his own financial problems could have been solved by his doing not one goddamned thing. Herb would simply have ignored the ransom demand, and the kidnappers would have done his dirty work for him. They'd kill Jane, and Herb could play the grieving husband legitimately. He'd have been rid of his wife and he'd be a rich man to boot, as soon as he inherited her money.

Instead, he'd acted like a complete ass—he'd reacted impulsively to a photograph in a catalog, cooked up this bone-headed scheme, smothered his wife, and planted her on a Big

Sur hillside. Now this Ellen woman had been kidnapped in Jane's place and things were quickly snowballing out of control. Damn that Ellen Merchant! Why did she have to sneak her goddamned sister into his house? That hadn't been their deal at all; Jane's double was supposed to stay there *alone* all week—he'd made that clear enough, hadn't he?—so nobody would know Jane was already dead.

"Excuse me, sir. Would you like something to drink?"

Herb's mental self-flagellation was interrupted by the flight attendant pushing the drink cart. "Huh?" he said stupidly, gazing up at the source of the voice.

"Something to drink, sir?" the tall, attractive brunette asked him again.

Herb figured he'd best stay away from alcohol; his head was already fuzzy enough. "Uh, yeah, coffee, please," he said. He pulled down his tray table and accepted the Styrofoam cup of steaming liquid he was handed, waving away the flight attendant's offer of cream and sugar.

There had to be some route around this, Herb told himself. There had to be one. Certainly it was just a matter of seeing things clearly, considering all the angles. He sipped his coffee slowly.

Maybe, just maybe there still was a way to make this fiasco work out to his benefit, he thought. There might be a way to force the kidnappers to kill Jane for him, after all. It was a huge gamble, but Herb was a gambler, wasn't he? The new plan that was forming in his mind just might work and, if it did, he could be far better off than before. His spirits began to lift as he worked out detail after detail in his mind.

First, of course, he wouldn't pay the ransom money. Not that he'd ever really intended to cough up a million bucks to save Ellen Merchant's ass. He didn't even know the bitch, plus she'd deceived him. No ransom money quickly equals one dead kidnap victim, right? Of course it did. Even in cases where families actually paid the ransom, the victim was frequently killed, if what Herb read in the papers was true.

So Ellen would die at the hands of the kidnappers who thought she was Jane Parkhurst Carmody. As next of kin, the grieving husband, Herb could identify Ellen's murdered body as that of his wife. A quick cremation of that body and, death certificate in hand, he would lay legal claim to his wife's sizable estate. And, in the meantime, surely the probate court would allow him to continue to collect the dividend and interest checks he and Jane had used to pay their living expenses over the past couple of years.

As his mind went over and over his new plan, Herb could see only one potentially fatal flaw—Claire Merchant. Obviously, Claire had to go if this thing was going to work. Yet she was the only person who could fill him in on the details about the kidnapping.

Claire presented a big obstacle, but Herb was confident he could overcome it. After all, there was nothing to connect her with him. He would simply have to con her into thinking he was doing everything possible to ransom her sister and, at the same time, make certain the woman hadn't told anyone else about the kidnapping, *especially the police.* After he was certain Ellen was dead, Herb could kill Claire and dispose of her body. Murder, like everything else, would be easier the second time around, and certainly the murder of a stranger, a stranger who'd virtually invaded his home, would be much, much easier than the murder of his wife had been.

After a quick cleansing of the house to remove any signs that the Merchant sisters had ever been there, Herb would be home free.

Home free and very, very soon he'd also be rich as sin.

14

"Spread that tarp out on the dirt next to her. I'll take the shovel, use it to roll her outta there," Lester Klemp ordered. He and his brother-in-law, Bobby Lee Brinton, were back at the cypress grove in mid-afternoon. This time, he'd left Pete locked inside his cabin while he took care of this grisly business.

"Jesus Christ, man, this mother sure stinks!" Bobby Lee said, holding his nose.

"Ain't her fault. You'd stink, too, you been dead for a while. Here, gimme that thing." Lester wrested the brown plastic tarp away from his brother-in-law's pudgy hands and began to spread it across the disturbed earth by himself. "There. You take the shovel and roll her out."

"Hell, no. I ain't touching no dead body, shovel or not. Bad enough Lorie talked me into letting you use my pickup to move it outta here."

"Always was a fucking chicken," Lester mumbled. He grabbed the shovel and used it as a wedge to lift the partially decomposed corpse from its shallow grave, then cantilevered it onto the tarp. When its head and feet were firmly entrenched on the brown plastic, he rolled the body over and over in the tarp until it was completely camouflaged. "You're sure as shit gonna help me carry her out to the truck," he declared.

"Hell, no, I'm—" Bobby Lee halted in mid-sentence as he caught the threatening look on Lester's face and noticed he was gripping the shovel with white knuckles. "She better be wrapped up damn good, that's all I can say," he agreed fi-

159

nally. "No way I'm putting my hands on no damn corpse."

Each of the men took an end of the rolled tarp and, breathing through their mouths to avoid smelling the rancid odor still emanating from their bundle, they made their way across the fields to the secluded spot where Bobby Lee had parked his pickup truck. They lifted the tarp and its contents onto the truck bed and secured it into place with an old rope.

"Let's get the hell outta here," Lester said, climbing onto the passenger seat. "We can drop her off the cliff at Hurricane Point."

"Hell, somebody's gonna find her there in no time!"

"Course they are, that's the idea."

"Whadya mean?" Bobby Lee asked, his habitual frown deepening.

"Look, dildo, this girl's somebody's wife or daughter, maybe even somebody's mother. Whoever the hell murdered her oughta pay, but I sure as shit ain't gonna let it be pinned on me."

As Bobby Lee drove, he kept sneaking looks at Lester, as though his wife's brother had smoked too much of his own crop and finally lost it completely.

"What?"

"We got our fingerprints all over that tarp, you dumb fuck," Bobby Lee pointed out. "Cops can get fingerprints off plastic, right? What if this fucking thing comes back to us?"

"Ain't gonna leave the tarp there, Bobby Lee. We roll her out, same as we rolled her in. Then we take the goddamn tarp home and bury it."

Claire had opened a can of tuna she'd found in one of the cupboards and was mixing its contents with mayonnaise from the refrigerator when the phone rang again. Startled, she nearly knocked over the mayonnaise jar. Were the kidnappers calling back already? It was barely three o'clock! Surely they didn't expect Herb to be here this quickly.

She wiped her hands on a towel, switched on the tape recorder and answered. "Carmody residence."

"Look, Mrs. Carmody," a deep male voice bellowed in her ear, "I'm outta patience here. You tell that fucking asshole you're married to he's been warned for the last time. He don't make his payment by the end of business today, the whole balance comes due—*or else*. No more fucking grace periods."

"What? Who is this?" Claire was so shocked by the tone of the call that she didn't even think to explain she was not Mrs. Carmody.

"Just tell Herb Kozlowski called. He knows. Seven grand, by the end of business today." He hung up.

Stunned, Claire checked to make sure her recorder had taped the call. It had. She replayed the recording twice, cringing as she listened to the obvious threat of violence this man who called himself Kozlowski had made.

Forgetting about her late lunch, Claire sank onto a chair, completely confused. Who were these strange Carmody people? They were supposed to be vacationing in Minnesota, but they'd gone somewhere else without even telling Ellen. The wife was supposedly kidnapped, yet Ellen had been snatched in her place. Herb apparently owed some thug named Kozlowski money but hadn't paid it on time—it obviously wasn't the friendly neighborhood banker she'd just captured on tape. It had to be a large debt, too, if seven thousand was merely an installment payment. Yet the Carmodys were loaded—Claire had seen evidence of that with her own eyes. So why hadn't Herb just paid whatever he owed?

She'd obviously been right to wonder about Ellen's apparent good luck in exchanging her tiny house for this spectacular one, Claire decided. There was plenty wrong with this deal. She just didn't know exactly what, not yet. And, as a result of this phone call, she was quickly losing confidence that Herb Carmody would be any help after he returned from Seattle. If he didn't even pay his debts to a goon like this Kozlowski fellow, what made her think he'd pay a million dollars to ransom Ellen?

There had to be another way she could investigate this thing by herself, Claire decided. If Herb was useless, maybe she could try to find Jane instead. It was possible Herb's wife might know who'd be likely to try to kidnap her—perhaps a former gardener or maintenance worker who'd seen first-hand how rich she was. Jane might be able to give Claire a lead. Where was she? Claire tried her best to recall what Herb had told her. Finally, it came to her—he'd said Jane had gone to visit her mother, that her mother had been taken ill.

Claire hurried back downstairs to the office and quickly located the stack of invoices from the Santa Barbara nursing home where Adeline Parkhurst lived. The phone number was right at the top of each bill. She pocketed the top one and hurried back upstairs to make her call from the kitchen. She would record all her calls from now on, she decided, just in case. That she was technically breaking the law meant nothing to her anymore, not under these circumstances. Hell, that Tripp woman got away with it and her sister's life hadn't been at stake. She put another fresh tape into the machine and shoved the Kozlowski tape into her briefcase, along with the others.

Claire quickly dialed the nursing home's phone number. When a receptionist answered, she asked, "May I speak with Mrs. Adeline Parkhurst, please?"

There was a pause. "I'm sorry, Mrs. Parkhurst isn't able to take phone calls. Who's calling, please?"

"My name is Claire Merchant and, actually, I'm trying to

reach Mrs. Parkhurst's daughter, Jane Carmody. I understand she's visiting her mother there." Even if Jane had no
suggestions about the kidnapping, Claire thought, she'd feel
better having warned her not to return home herself. She was
no longer sure she could trust Herb to have done it, promise
or no promise.

There was another, briefer pause on the phone. "Can you
hold a minute?" the receptionist asked.

"Certainly."

When the line was picked up again, Claire heard a different voice. "Ms. Merchant? This is Dina, the head nurse on
Mrs. Parkhurst's floor. Can I help you?"

"As I told the receptionist, I'm trying to reach Mrs. Parkhurst's daughter, Jane Carmody. I understand she's there."

"I'm afraid not," Dina told her. "We haven't seen Mrs.
Carmody in at least a year."

"But her husband told me her mother was sick, that Jane
had gone to visit her."

"Her mother certainly *is* sick," Dina said. "Adeline has
Alzheimer's disease. But she hasn't recognized her family
members in at least three years, so Mrs. Carmody pretty
much stopped coming to visit her. I understand she moved
away, somewhere up near San Francisco."

"I—I guess I misunderstood," Claire said, baffled. "Sorry
to have bothered you."

"Oh, it's no problem. Maybe Mrs. Carmody's on her way
here. If she arrives, should I tell her you're trying to reach
her?"

"Yes, please," Claire replied. "Will you tell her to call
home right away, that Claire Merchant very much needs to
talk to her?"

As she hung up the phone and shut off the tape recorder, a
chill ran down Claire's spine. Which one of the Carmodys

was lying? Had Herb lied about his wife's whereabouts, or had Jane told her husband she was visiting her mother and then gone somewhere else, perhaps with her lover?

Yet the latter scenario didn't make much sense. What about the flowers that had arrived for Jane on Monday? What had the accompanying card said? "With all my love," that was it. If Jane had a lover and had sneaked off with him, the man hardly would've sent flowers to her home while they were off together on a clandestine outing. And, if Herb thought Jane was in Santa Barbara, he wouldn't have sent her the flowers, either.

After considering the possibilities, Claire found herself inclined to believe it was Herb who wasn't telling the truth, rather than his wife. If he made a habit of hanging around with men like Kozlowski, who knew what sort of person he was? Yet why didn't he want her to know where Jane had gone?

Maybe she should go to the police after all, Claire thought, realizing for the first time that she could actually be in danger from Herb Carmody, or from his violence-threatening friends, once he returned.

But if she went to the police, her action could well cause Ellen's death. And if she moved out of the house for her own safety, she'd lose access to any clue that could lead her to her sister's whereabouts.

No, she couldn't take either of those routes. She'd simply have to chance that she could protect herself from Herb Carmody and his cohorts if he turned out not to be what he claimed, if instead of offering help, he tried to harm her.

Claire walked into the bedroom and took the metal box down from the shelf in Jane's closet. She lifted the stack of papers and found the small, pearl-handled gun. Much as she hated to think about having to use this thing, it made her feel she might have a fighting chance if—

If what? She wasn't sure exactly what she was afraid of. But after all the violence she'd seen in her lifetime, both first- and secondhand, Claire was anything but naive. She tucked the gun into the pocket of her jeans and put the box back on the shelf.

Certainly it couldn't hurt to be prepared.

Ellen lay prone once more, her ear pressed against the rough, dirty sub-flooring of her prison room. Her bones ached after lying here for nearly an hour and her nose itched from the dust, but at least she'd learned a few things for her trouble.

One of her two captors was called Sid, she now knew, and the other was Harry or Barry or Larry—she couldn't hear well enough through the plywood to be certain. And both men appeared to know Herb Carmody fairly well, although Ellen had the impression that Herb had no idea they were the ones who'd kidnapped his "wife."

Harry or Barry or whatever his name was did a lot of worrying out loud, expressing concern that somehow Herb would figure out who they were and turn them in to the cops.

"Shit, will ya get off that one-note tune?" Ellen heard Sid reply. "I told ya fifty times—Herb figures it out sooner'n we planned, all we gotta do is maybe cut him a bigger chunk of the ransom money. He's gonna keep his lip zipped. Hell, we're saving his ass here, right? Ain't like it's his money he's gonna be paying out. Belongs to that stingy bitch, and she ain't even willing to bail him out with Kozlowski. Some love story they got going!"

The voices faded again. Ellen stayed in position for a few minutes longer, waiting for the conversation to resume.

A loud knock on her door startled her. Her heart leaping

wildly, she jumped to her feet and shoved the carpet and pad back into place as fast as she could. If Sid and his pal found out she'd been eavesdropping, they'd undoubtedly kill her on the spot!

"What?" she called out in a shaky voice. With her feet, she quickly smoothed out a telltale wrinkle in the section of carpet she'd lifted and prayed nobody looked at that corner too closely.

"Got your dinner, Mrs. Carmody. Get in the bathroom and close the door. Keep your eyes shut. You know the drill."

"All right," Ellen said, following her captors' instructions.

As she stood inside the bathroom, she realized how close she'd come to being caught red-handed and began to tremble all over. She couldn't stop shivering until she heard the outer door slam shut once more, the signal that she was free to come out of the bathroom.

She saw another plastic tray perched on the couch; this time, it was holding a plate of lukewarm canned hash and a fistful of potato chips. Another unopened can of Coca-Cola rounded out the meal her kidnappers had provided for her.

Ellen picked up the plastic fork and poked at her food. She'd felt the pangs of hunger only a few minutes earlier, but her close brush with discovery had killed her appetite. She put down the fork, held her head in her hands, and dissolved into tears.

Deputy Christy Jimenez stood a few feet away from her squad car, just inside the yellow tape that cordoned off the crime scene. She gazed out at the churning gray sea while the rescue team lifted the body, strapped to a gurney suspended by thick ropes, over the side of the Hurricane Point cliff and into the parking area. She already knew the corpse was female—that was the reason her colleagues had called her to the spot where a tourist had reported finding a dead body. Protocol required that the initial search of a female corpse be done by a female deputy and, this time, she'd been elected.

"She's all yours, Christy," Deputy Zeke Danielson, the head of today's investigation team, told her. "Do your thing." Was that a sneer she detected on his leathery middle-aged face, a hint of glee that she, and not he, would have to body search this partially decomposed cadaver?

In contrast to Zeke's joviality, she saw Deputy Gino Vitelli cross himself and say a brief prayer, as was his habit with every fatality they investigated. Nobody ever gave Gino any trouble or dared imply *he* was too soft for the job. But then, Gino was a six-foot-tall, two-hundred-ten-pound male, while she was merely a slender five-foot-four-inch female.

Maybe she was just being paranoid, Christy decided as she took her time pulling on her rubber gloves. Most men in the sheriff's department had had plenty of time to become used to having female colleagues. Of course, that didn't mean they didn't enjoy taunting them on occasion, and she'd been the butt of plenty of practical jokes during her five years on the job.

Refusing to let the men surrounding her see how much the ravaged condition of the corpse—this one had been dead for at least several days—repulsed her, Christy took a deep breath and thrust her gloved fingers into what was left of the dead woman's pants pockets. Her tailored slacks appeared to be made of fine gray wool, but they'd been so shredded and soiled by animals and her slide down the cliff-side that very little of the fabric remained. Both pockets were empty. "No wallet or ID on the vic," Christy reported.

Next, she looked for any labels the woman's clothing might have. Forcing down the stomach acid that kept rising in her throat, Christy rolled the body over. The shirt the dead woman wore had been pale green, probably silk, but, like her slacks, it was badly soiled and in tatters. If either garment had ever had a manufacturer's label or a dry cleaner's mark, it was long gone.

Shielding the corpse from her colleagues' prying eyes—Christy figured this poor dead woman deserved what little dignity she could manage to give her—she pulled the back of the victim's shirt upward and the waist of her slacks downward so she could check her underwear. Only her peach-colored underpants, which also appeared to be silk, held any information that might lead to an identification.

"There's part of a label still intact on her panties," Christy said. She squinted at it. She could barely make out the words, "—ade for Jane Carm—." "The panties appear to be custom-made. Looks like the vic's first name might be Jane."

"*That* sure narrows it down," Zeke said, barely suppressing another mocking grin.

Christy straightened up and pulled off her gloves. Choosing to ignore her colleague's teasing, she told him, "Might be enough left of her fingers for the coroner to print her, but I wouldn't guarantee it."

As the gurney was lifted into the van for transportation to the Coroner's office in Salinas, Christy said her own silent prayer for this woman who'd died violently. Whether "Jane" had died as the result of an accident, suicide or murder, she couldn't yet be absolutely certain but, if Christy were a betting woman, she'd put her money on murder. This one had all the earmarks of a dump job. Whatever the cause of her death, poor "Jane Carm—" surely had been cut down long before her appointed time.

"So long, Jane," Christy whispered under her breath as she climbed back into the driver's seat of her squad car.

"Hope you had a good life . . . as long as it lasted."

In downtown Sausalito, the seaside tourist town only one ferry stop away from Tiburon, Frank Washington, a tow truck driver for the city, hooked up the dark green Jaguar and cranked its front end three feet off the pavement. The Jag, parked on Bridgeway Boulevard, Sausalito's main drag, had been ticketed four times in the past twenty-four hours. It was now headed for the police storage lot, where it would stay, collecting a daily storage charge, until its owner bailed it out.

Because this was such an expensive car, Frank knew the meter maid had checked with area police departments to determine whether it had been reported stolen before summoning him.

"Goddamned yuppie scum," he muttered under his breath as he turned on his rig's flashing lights and pulled out into traffic with his load. "Think they own the streets, can park anywhere they fucking well please."

Frank towed away an average of a dozen expensive cars a week from this area, and frequently he was subjected to irate tirades by the vehicles' wealthy, self-important owners when they finally showed up at the police storage lot to retrieve them. Somehow, they all seemed to figure *their* cars would never be towed, no matter how long they over-parked. One guy even had the audacity to yell at Frank, "You should've known I was good for the fines. If I can afford a Maserati, I'm no fucking deadbeat, right? You better not have put one scratch on my car, mister, or I'll have your job!"

He'd better not get a shitload of that kind of attitude from the owner of this Jag, Frank decided. He was in no mood.

Neither Frank nor the meter maid had looked under the driver's seat of the green Jaguar, where they would have found its keys, nor had they looked inside the trunk, which

169

contained two bags of rotting groceries and Ellen Merchant's purse, from which all the cash she'd saved for her trip to California had been stolen.

Claire became hyper-alert as she heard the sound of a car pulling into the circular driveway, followed by the slamming of its door. She peeked out the kitchen window and saw a Yellow Cab pulling away from the house. A moment later, she heard a key turn in front door's lock.

"Hello!" a now-familiar male voice called. "Anybody home?"

"I'm here, Mr. Carmody," Claire responded. She swallowed her apprehension, patted the small gun in her pocket for reassurance, and headed for the entryway.

Herb put down his suitcase and carry-on and held out his hand. "Claire Merchant, I presume?" He flashed a smile at her, revealing even white teeth and deep blue eyes. "I'm Herb Carmody."

Claire nodded solemnly and shook the tall, blond man's hand. She noticed he had the broad, strong shoulders of a one-time athlete, but was now slightly paunchy, as though he'd stopped working out a few years back. Still, Herb was a handsome man near her own age, a man she might have been attracted to under much different circumstances.

"I—I'm glad you made it back so fast," she said, not completely certain how to proceed. She tried her best not to appear too suspicious, yet her natural instincts kept telling her this guy was going to be trouble.

"Yeah, I was lucky enough to get onto one of the early shuttle flights," Herb agreed. "Did the kidnappers call again?"

Claire was relieved not to have to make small talk with the owner of this house. "Yes, and I managed to record the call," she reported. "Unfortunately, I didn't get this guy's first call on tape, just the follow-up." She led Herb into the kitchen, where she took the cassette she'd marked with the word, "Kidnapper," and the time and date of the call, from her briefcase and snapped it into the recorder. She hit PLAY and listened again to her own voice and that of one of Ellen's captors. "Does that man's voice sound familiar?" she asked Herb when the brief recording had ended. "Could it be anybody you know?"

Herb shook his head, perhaps a bit too quickly, Claire thought. "No, nobody I recognize, that's for sure. Sounds like he's going to call back again, though."

"He'll have to, if he wants the ransom money."

"Guess I'll go unpack and wait until he does, then," Herb told her. "You staying in the guest room?"

"I have been," Claire said. "Ellen was using the master bedroom, but I moved her things into the guest room with mine, and I put fresh sheets on your bed."

"Thoughtful."

"I hope it's all right if I stay here until we get my sister back," Claire said as she removed the cassette from the recorder and set it on the table.

"Of course," Herb told her, cranking up his charm another level. "Absolutely. Wouldn't even *think* of letting you leave, certainly not in the middle of this horrible thing with your sister. And, by the way, don't worry about my wife coming back early. When I told Jane what happened, she promised to stay away for as long as it takes to make sure Ellen is safe."

Claire felt an icicle of fear slither down her spine. "So your wife is going to stay at her mother's until this is resolved?" she asked Herb, watching his face intently.

"Right. Believe me, it's not a problem, Claire. Jane was

planning to stay the full week, anyway."

The man was good, Claire decided, as her instincts about him were instantly confirmed. He really was very good. His glance had barely flicked away from hers as he told her what she knew full well was a boldface lie, and his facial expression had remained completely benign, virtually unreadable. "That's a relief," she said, hoping she was as good a liar as Herb, although somehow she doubted she'd had nearly as much practice. "Oh, I almost forgot, Mr. Carmody—"

"Herb, please."

"Herb, then. You got another call, from a man named Kozinski or Kaminski—no, Kozlowski, that was it. Mr. Kozlowski called."

This time, Claire noticed that Herb's breath caught slightly and he turned a shade paler before responding. "Say what he wanted?" he asked.

She felt as if his eyes were boring holes into hers. "Just that you should call him back," she said, fighting to keep her demeanor as normal as possible. "Said you'd know what it was about."

"Thanks," Herb said, picking up his suitcase. "I'll call him later. Don't want to tie up the phone in case the kidnappers call back. For now, I'll go unpack my bags."

Herb tossed the suitcase and carry-on bag onto the freshly made bed but made no move to open them. He was almost positive he'd recognized the voice on that tape. It sounded exactly like Sid Balzarian, the Elvis Presley wannabe who'd driven him home from Jocks that night he'd gotten so drunk.

Would Balzarian try a dumb-ass stunt like this kidnapping thing? Herb had heard rumors that the guy with the graying duck-tail haircut was into the smalltime con whenever he was short of gambling money, that he had a talent for swindling elderly people out of their paltry savings or running the occasional pyramid scheme and not getting caught. But a kidnapping for ransom? Did Sid have that kind of balls?

Either way, it sure couldn't hurt to find out where the old boy hung out when he wasn't slurping a beer at Jocks.

Herb picked up the bedside phone and began calling his gambling buddies. Surely somebody would be able to tell him how to contact Balzarian.

As she stood in the kitchen, Claire's mind raced. She was now more nervous than ever about staying here with the clearly duplicitous Herb Carmody, yet she could see no other choice. She removed all the cassettes except the one she'd already played for Herb and her work interviews from her briefcase. She would hide the rest of them somewhere else, perhaps in her car. Certainly she didn't want Herb to find out she knew any more about him than he wanted her to.

Her gaze flicked to the telephone and she noticed a tiny flashing red light, indicating that the line was in use. So much for Herb's not wanting to tie up the phone. He was making a call from the bedroom. As fast as she could, Claire put a fresh tape into her recorder and hit the record button.

Within three quick calls, Herb had located a telephone number for Sid Balzarian. He dialed it.

"Hello. Balzarian residence." The quivering voice seemed to be that of an elderly woman.

"Hi," Herb said. "Sid home?"

"Sorry, no," the woman said. "Sidney's away all week."

"Oh, dear," Herb said. "I was really hoping to reach him. This is, uh, his friend Tom. Is this Sid's wife?"

The old woman laughed. "Goodness, no. I'm Sidney's

173

mother. He doesn't have a *wife*." She said the final word as though it would be the strangest thing in the world for the middle-aged Sid to be married.

"Oops, sorry, Mrs. Balzarian, your voice sounded so *young*," Herb said, laying it on thick. "Your son and I know each other from Jocks—you know, the sports bar. I've got an extra ticket for the playoffs—they're terribly hard to get—and I thought Sid might like to go."

"The playoffs? You mean baseball?"

"Right, San Francisco and New York."

"Oh, I'm sure he'd be thrilled. My Sidney's a real big baseball fan."

"The thing is, though, I can't hold onto the ticket much longer. Is there some way I can contact Sid today?"

"You might try calling him up at his Uncle Edwin's house in Petaluma. He's spending the week up there, fixing up the old place so it's ready to be sold, now the probate's near ready to close."

"You have that phone number, Mrs. Balzarian?"

"Of course, Tom." The old woman recited it and Herb copied it down on a pad of paper he kept in his nightstand drawer.

He dialed the number as soon as he got the old woman off the line.

The phone was answered on the third ring. "Hello."

Herb disguised his voice and asked, "Is Buck there?"

"No Buck here. You got the wrong number."

As he hung up the phone, Herb felt absolutely certain the voice he'd just heard on the other end was the same one Claire had recorded earlier. The idiot who'd thought he'd kidnapped Jane was none other than Sid Balzarian, small time con artist. Herb was glad he was hidden away in the bedroom—he couldn't stop grinning about the huge piece of good luck this whole fiasco was turning out to be for him.

In Salinas, the Coroner finished his autopsy on the corpse found in Big Sur. Judging by the extent of decomposition of the unidentified red-head's body, he concluded she'd been dead at least four or five days, and she hadn't died at the spot where she'd been found. Instead, she'd died of suffocation and her body was dumped on the cliff-side postmortem.

He'd already tagged and bagged the shredded garments the victim had been wearing when she was found and turned them over to the district attorney's office, in case murder charges ever were filed. Now, the Coroner quickly passed on his conclusions to the Sheriff's deputies investigating this murder. He knew the media were already on the story, waiting to be briefed.

The one piece of luck the Coroner'd had that might lead him to an identification of the body was the partial thumbprint he'd been able to lift from her right thumb. If she'd been a licensed California driver, that thumbprint would be on file with the DMV in Sacramento.

When she noticed the flashing red light on the telephone had ceased, Claire quickly removed the cassette from the recorder, marked it with an unobtrusive X, and replaced it with a fresh one. She dared not listen to Herb's clandestine conversation now, not when he could emerge from the bedroom at any moment.

Almost immediately, the phone rang. Claire hit RECORD. But before she could pick up the receiver, the flashing red light came on again. Herb had answered the call in the bedroom.

"Hello," Herb said.

"Herb Carmody?"

"Yeah, who's this?"

"We got your wife. You want her back, you put together a million bucks—small bills, none of 'em marked—and she don't get hurt. Got it?"

Herb was now doubly certain he was talking to Sid Balzarian, but he had to play along. "I—I'll pay you, but I want assurance Jane's not already dead," he said.

"That other woman figured you'd wanna talk to her, so we got her right here. Hear for yourself, we ain't harmed a hair on her pretty red head—not yet."

"Herb? Herb, is that you?" Herb recognized Ellen Merchant's voice, although it was far weaker and less assured now than it had been when they'd spoken about the house exchange a couple of weeks ago.

"Yes, Jane," he said, sticking to his script, "it's me. Are you all right, hon? They haven't hurt you, have they?"

"I—I'm just scared, really scared, but I'm not hurt. You've got to figure out how to pay them the money they want or—" Ellen's voice was cut off abruptly, in mid-sentence.

"She's said enough," Herb heard Sid say to someone on his end of the line. "Get her back upstairs!" At least the Merchant woman had the common sense to play along, to let these yahoos believe she was Jane, Herb thought. That could only work in his favor, in the end.

"Look, Carmody, we're basically peaceful guys here," Sid said into the phone. "You get our million bucks together, we don't have us no more trouble, right?"

"There's just one problem," Herb said, thinking fast. If he flat-out refused to pay the ransom money, Balzarian *might* kill Ellen but, then again, he might not. And, if he didn't, Herb's plans would slide downhill faster than those Olympic bobsledders he'd won a bundle on four years ago.

"Don't go trying to con us, Carmody, I'm warning you."

"I'm not, believe me. Problem is, everything is in my wife's name, even the house. It's all her inheritance from her father. Without Jane's signature, I can't get together ten thousand bucks, never mind a million. She's going to have to sign papers before I can pay you."

"She call her bank, authorize you to get the dough."

"No, that won't work," Herb insisted. "The bank's going to require my wife's signature. Plus, she doesn't have a million dollars sitting in a bank account. Most of her wealth is in stocks. I'm going to need her to sign some papers before I can sell them."

There was a long pause. Herb felt confident that Balzarian would buy his story. Not only was it true, but he'd complained about his money situation to this little twerp before now.

"Okay, okay, I hear what you're saying," Sid said, finally. "Just don't try nothing funny. Get together whatever papers you need. Take 'em to your gallery, the one in Tiburon, and wait there. We'll call you with directions where to go."

"It's going to take me an hour or so to get everything together," Herb said, doing his best to stall. He had to have enough time to find out where Sid's Uncle Edwin's house was located before he could put the next stage of his plan into action.

"Give ya exactly one hour. You're late, your old lady has a fatal accident." Sid hung up.

Herb opened the top drawer of the nightstand and pulled out the thick North Bay telephone directory, quickly thumbing through its pages. *Thank you, God,* he thought— *here it was.* Edwin Balzarian was listed at a Petaluma address, and his phone number was the same one Sid's mother had given Herb. Apparently the old boy hadn't yet been dead long enough for his name to be removed from the phone directory. Herb jotted down the address and stuffed the scrap of paper into his pants pocket.

He grabbed the gray metal box from Jane's closet shelf—he'd searched through it many times before, during some of the times his wife was attending one of her fundraisers, or was off having her hair done, or her legs waxed, or whatever filthy rich women like her did when they left their fancy houses. But this time, he wasn't interested in the stack of financial documents the box held—he had no intention of using any of them to pay Ellen Merchant's ransom. Instead, he was searching for the small pearl-handled gun he knew Jane kept hidden there.

Damn! The gun was gone. She must have decided to hide it somewhere else. Still, if Herb couldn't find Jane's own gun, it wasn't exactly the end of the world. He had other options. He headed downstairs to the den and, using the key he carried on his key ring, unlocked the gun cabinet. He ignored the rifles and shotguns hanging on display behind the glass doors—they were far too noticeable for what he had in mind. Instead, he lifted a hidden panel at the bottom of the cabinet and removed a loaded .38 caliber handgun from its compact storage space. He tucked it into the waistband of his slacks and pulled down his sweater far enough to conceal it from view.

Then, grabbing a few random file folders from the home office next door, he headed back upstairs.

"You tape the call that came in?" Herb asked Claire as he came into the kitchen.

She nodded. "Was it the kidnapper again?"

"Right." Herb was pleased that this tape would be yet another piece of evidence he could use to prove Jane had been kidnapped. "Keep that tape safe along with the other one, Claire, and stay in the house until I get back. You never know, these guys could call again."

Claire's gaze darted to Herb's face. "Are you going somewhere?" she asked anxiously.

He held up the folders. "Here's the deal. I told them Jane has to sign these papers before I can get hold of the million dollars—it has to come from her inheritance, which I can't touch by myself. They're going to call me at my gallery here in town in about half an hour, give me directions where to take the papers."

"But Ellen can't sign those!"

"Don't worry. Trust me, Claire, this is just a ruse to keep these guys occupied for a while, to give me some time to get the cash together. I'll call Jane from the gallery, let her know what's happening. She can notify her bank, give the okay for me to get the money out of her accounts tomorrow morning. All we're doing is stalling for time and reassuring the kidnappers they've got the real Jane Carmody."

"Okay, okay, I guess that makes sense," Claire said, anxiously twisting a lock of hair around her finger. "You're sure Jane will go along with this? I mean, a million dollars—"

"Hey, it could've been her, grabbed off the streets like that, right? Believe me, Jane's not going to gripe about ponying up a million bucks under these circumstances. Later on, after Ellen's safe, we can go to the police, maybe get our money back."

"I certainly hope you're right. This is Ellen's *life* we're talking about."

Herb reached over and gripped Claire's shoulder firmly. "Trust me, Claire," he said, examining her face for any signs of rebellion, "everything's going to be all right. Just stay here in case there are any more phone calls, and I'll be back just as soon as I can."

179

Herb opened the garage door, maneuvered his Jeep past Claire's old junker, and headed downhill. As he reached the stop sign at Tiburon Boulevard and signaled his turn, he switched on the radio.

" . . . body of an unidentified woman found in Big Sur earlier today," he heard a reporter say. He sucked in his breath. *No! It couldn't be, not this fast! Not now!* "A Monterey County Sheriff's deputy rescue team recovered the body from a steep incline at Hurricane Point . . ." Herb exhaled again, his hands on the steering wheel shaking wildly from the sudden fright.

So it wasn't Jane after all. It couldn't be. This body had been thrown off a cliff. Whoever this dead woman was, Herb reassured himself, she definitely was not Jane.

15

The fax machine in the Monterey County Coroner's Office rang twice, then whirred and spit out a single sheet of paper. Secretary Lydia Tyler grabbed it as soon as it was printed.

"Bingo!" she said as she realized it was a reply to the query she'd faxed to the DMV a couple of hours ago. Sacramento had found a match for the Big Sur murder victim's thumbprint. The dead woman was now identified as Jane Parkhurst Carmody, age thirty, five-feet-seven, one hundred and eighteen pounds, red hair, green eyes. The DMV supplied her Tiburon address as well.

Lydia quickly phoned the Sheriff's office and relayed the DMV's information to Deputy Zeke Danielson, the primary on the murder case.

"Hey, nice going, Lydia," Zeke told her. "Owe you one. I'll call up to Tiburon right away, ask the local PD to contact the vic's family. Any of those media goons call your office, you keep your lip zipped, okay? I'm not releasing the dead woman's identity until her family's been notified."

As soon as she saw Herb pull out of the garage driving the Jeep, Claire played the tapes she'd made of his phone calls. Who the hell was Sid Balzarian, she wondered after listening to the first few calls, and why was Herb trying to find him? But after she heard Herb call Balzarian's mother and pretend to be Sid's friend Tom, a theory began to form in her mind. She made a note of the Petaluma phone number the old woman gave him.

Claire found the voice of the man who answered the final

181

call on Herb's first tape, the one in which he asked to speak with somebody named Buck, very familiar. Tingling with anticipation, she plugged in the second tape and hit PLAY. Her heart flip-flopped as she heard her sister's voice—poor Ellen sounded so frightened, so alone! Yet she was still alive and apparently unharmed, which gave Claire new faith that somehow they would survive this ordeal.

She played parts of both tapes again, listening carefully until she was positive the voice at the end of the first tape matched that of the kidnapper. She no longer had any doubt that one of the men who'd snatched Ellen was named Sidney Balzarian. Who Balzarian was, she had no idea. But she was absolutely certain of one other thing—Herb Carmody knew this man, and he'd lied straight to her face about that vitally important fact.

Claire already knew, of course, that Herb also had lied about his wife's whereabouts—Jane's mother's nursing home told her directly that Jane was not there, that she hadn't been there in months. It was entirely possible, Claire realized, that every single word out of Herb's mouth had been untrue, although she had no idea why. She'd learned to trust her reporter's instincts, and all of them had been alerted by the number of times the man preceded his statements with phrases like "Believe me . . ." or "Trust me . . ." She'd learned long ago that such unnecessary reassurances were classic signs the speaker was about to tell a whopper.

Had Herb really spoken to Jane at all? Did either of the Carmodys have the least intention of paying the ransom money? Claire couldn't help but have extremely strong doubts.

Still, she had no real clue about what Herb was up to. Perhaps he had a plan to rescue Ellen without handing over any of the money, she speculated. But, if that were the case, wouldn't he have shared that plan with her? She was Ellen's sister, for god's sake, the kidnapped woman's only family!

No, there was something else going on here, something sinister and terrifying, perhaps even something involving that Kozlowski guy and his thinly veiled threats of violence. Claire vowed not to rest until she found out what it was.

She peered out the front window to reassure herself that Herb wasn't returning to the house, then hurried into the master bedroom and took the gray metal box off Jane's closet shelf. A glance through the financial documents it held showed her nothing had been removed since she'd last looked inside. Obviously, if Herb really was carrying any financial papers when he left the house, he hadn't taken them from here. Yet, in Claire's earlier search of the house, she'd found no additional records of Jane's financial holdings, not so much as a checkbook.

Claire picked up the bedroom telephone and hit REDIAL. When her call was answered, she recognized Balzarian's voice on the other end. She wanted to scream at the man to let her sister go, to abandon his ill-fated scheme, but that would be incredibly stupid, not to mention counterproductive. Instead, she hung up without saying a word.

Back in the kitchen, Claire used her laptop to log onto the Internet. Within a few minutes, she'd accessed the reverse telephone directory used by journalists, located a Petaluma address for Edwin Balzarian, and copied map directions from Tiburon to the Sonoma County house. She felt a bit nauseous as she realized this address might well be where Ellen was being kept prisoner.

Maybe her best move would be to call the police right now, Claire told herself, to hand over the information she'd gathered and let the professionals handle things from here on out. But what if the kidnappers were staying in Petaluma, yet keeping Ellen elsewhere? What if they'd moved her after phoning their last demand? What if they were taking her along to wherever they planned to pick up those financial papers, the ones Herb claimed she had to sign? What if one of them was watching this house right now?

No, Claire decided, she still couldn't risk bringing the police into this, not with Ellen's very survival at stake. She glanced at the clock on the kitchen wall. Twenty minutes had elapsed since Herb left the house, almost fifty since the kidnappers' last call. If Balzarian kept his word about phoning the Tiburon gallery in an hour, she might still have time. If she hurried, she should be able to follow Herb as he left the gallery after Sid's call and tail him to his destination. Maybe then she'd be able to figure out what he was doing, as well as where Ellen was being held.

Claire grabbed her notes and the tape cassettes and slid them, along with the little pearl-handled gun, into her purse. Slinging the bag over her shoulder, she hurried out to her car. She looked around as she drove away from the house, but saw no one who seemed to be watching her. If somebody was, she hoped he'd think she was just the maid on her way home after a day's work.

As she hurried downhill toward town, Claire spotted a Tiburon PD cruiser approaching from the opposite direction. She hit the brakes—the last thing she needed right now was a speeding ticket, particularly while she was carrying a concealed weapon!—but the cop ignored her. She glanced in her rearview mirror and saw the squad car continuing its trek uphill, retracing the route she'd just traveled.

As she reached Tiburon Boulevard and turned toward town, Claire couldn't help feeling an additional jolt of apprehension as she wondered just where that police car might be heading.

Detective George Vanheusen pulled into the circular

driveway in front of the Carmody house. He hated making house calls like this one—having to tell some poor mother her daughter was dead, or explain to a husband that his wife had been murdered, then add the bombshell that the grieving relatives would be required to undergo intensive police questioning over the coming days. Yet it was part of the job he'd signed on to do.

He rang the doorbell and waited. When no one had answered after several minutes and two more tries on the doorbell, the detective figured it might be out of order. There were lights on inside, which generally indicated somebody was home. He tried banging on the door, long and hard.

Strange, George thought. There still was no answer. Perhaps the blazing lights were part of the Carmodys' security system, a ruse to make burglars think the place was occupied when in fact the owners were away. Unlike their local police, people who could afford a house like this one, probably worth a good three to four million in today's hot real estate market, hardly had worries about paying an inflated electric bill.

Unless she'd been abducted and murdered from this house while its lights were left burning. But it was much too soon to conclude that sort of thing. And George's impression was that the late Jane Carmody hadn't lived here alone. There was a Herb Carmody, probably her husband, listed at this address in the phone book. On the other hand, the property records indicated she owned this place by herself, so maybe Herb was her father or her son rather than her husband.

George took a business card out of his wallet, wrote, "Urgent! Please call as soon as possible," on the back, and tucked it into the space between the front door and its frame. If he hadn't received a phone call within a couple of hours, he decided, he'd make another trip up the hill from town.

Waves II was closed and dark, Claire saw, as she pulled into the public parking lot serving the art gallery, an adjacent real estate office, and a law firm. The handful of cars there did not include Herb's Jeep. Maybe there was an employee parking lot around the back of the long, low brown building, she thought, telling herself the gallery's offices were probably in the back as well. Nervous that Herb might spot her, she drove around the side of the building. There were, indeed, several parking spots along a high security fence back here, but only one of them was occupied, by a new white Lexus SUV. Except for a security light above the back door, the rear portion of Waves II was just as dark and deserted as the front.

Herb Carmody was nowhere in sight.

Claire's dashboard clock reassured her that she'd made it to the gallery with a few minutes to spare. Unless Sid Balzarian had called early and Herb had already left his business to bring the kidnapper those financial papers . . .

Somehow, Claire didn't think so. Her strong suspicion was that the duplicitous Mr. Carmody had never intended being here to take that call. He probably hadn't phoned his wife, either. His promise to pay the million-dollar ransom undoubtedly was sheer bullshit as well.

But where had he gone? And why?

Claire saw only one course of action left. She couldn't trust Balzarian not to kill Ellen as soon as he realized Herb intended to shine him on about the money. She had no choice but to head straight for Petaluma.

Herb found the place where Sid's uncle had lived and died about a mile outside the town of Petaluma. He drove slowly past the seedy yellow two-story dwelling, noticing that half its windows were boarded up, although there were lights burning brightly on the lower floor. The shrubs around the foundation were yellow and bedraggled, badly in need of water and care, and the lawn was long since dead. Sid's mother had better think again—her son obviously had spent about as much time fixing up this dump during the past week as Herb had spent running in the Kentucky Derby!

Luckily, the house was surrounded by trees and perched in the middle of a half-acre lot. Herb had feared that neighbors might have an easy view of the place, a complication he didn't need, but his newfound luck was still holding fast. As he cruised past, he noted that people seemed to be home at two of the houses across the road.

It was dusk and there was no sense attracting unnecessary attention by walking down the road when he might easily be seen by a neighbor, Herb decided. There was no real reason to hurry. If Balzarian took out Ellen Merchant before he arrived to do the job himself, all the better. Herb would be left with only the clean-up problem.

He turned around and drove past the house once more, then parked about a hundred yards down the road, under the limbs of a sheltering eucalyptus tree, and waited for darkness to fall. It wouldn't be much longer now.

The fog was blowing in off the bay as Claire headed north on Highway 101, proceeding according to the directions she'd copied off her computer's screen. She took the turnoff for Petaluma but angled south well before reaching the town's center. Her directions indicated that the Balzarian house was almost in the countryside, located about a mile from the border of Petaluma.

It took her another fifteen minutes to find the stretch of road where the house was supposed to be. It was both foggy and close to dark by now, as Claire drove past several old homes, wondering with a combination of fear and foolishness whether her sister really was nearby, or if she'd come here on a wild goose chase. She slowed down, squinting at the faded numbers painted on the roadside mailboxes as she searched for the right address.

As the numbers on the mailboxes grew larger, Claire spotted Herb's Jeep parked at the side of the road under a huge tree and her heart leapt into her throat. She turned her face away, in case Herb might be sitting inside his car, and sped past, hoping he hadn't recognized her or her car. The Jeep served as an instant confirmation that she'd come to the right place, but there was no advantage in letting its driver know she'd followed him here.

Claire drove straight past the boarded-up yellow house and slowed down again only after she realized the house numbers were now higher than the address she was seeking. She pulled over to the side of the road, turned off her engine, and waited until she could think calmly and clearly about what to do next.

Now that she was actually here, Claire figured, she'd have to take a closer look at the Balzarian house and try to determine whether her sister was imprisoned there. After she'd confirmed her hunch, perhaps she could ask a neighbor to summon the police.

Shivering in the damp evening air, Claire grabbed her windbreaker off the backseat and slipped it on, then tucked the small gun into her right pocket and her car keys into her left. She switched off the interior light of the car so it wouldn't flash on when she opened the door, climbed out, and crept back along the road.

Herb crouched down outside the living room window of

the yellow house, his .38 gripped in his hand. Through the thin, cheap window glass, he could hear two men talking inside. One, he was pretty sure, was Sid, and the other guy sounded like Barry O'Farrell, Sid's buddy from Jocks. As far as he could tell, it was only the two of them there.

"Won't be long now," he heard Sid say. "Gonna be in fat city, you and me, just like that bitch upstairs. Up for a trip to Vegas when this is over? Wouldn't mind increasing my little nest egg with a wager or two."

"Yeah, sure. But ain't you forgetting something? Asshole didn't answer the phone on time, way you told him. Maybe he don't plan on paying nothing to get his old lady back."

"Hey, loosen up. Probably just taking Herb a little longer than he figured to get them papers together. Million bucks is a lotta dough. So I'll call him again in a couple minutes."

"And what you gonna do if Herb don't give a damn about his rich bitch wife, huh? Maybe he figures—she's dead, so much the better for him. What then?"

"So then we call and clue him in on the real deal, about his cut of the mil and all. He ain't gonna turn down enough green to get out from under Kozlowski."

"Jesus, Sid, you're gonna fucking ID us over the phone?"

"Lighten up, pal. Only if it comes to that."

Herb stood back from the window and looked around. There was no passing traffic and the neighborhood still seemed quiet. Apparently Ellen was being kept somewhere upstairs; that was good. This operation was best done in manageable stages. He'd need to find a second gun to kill her with, one of Sid's weapons, and that would be much easier to do after the two men were dead.

He screwed up his courage. No point in being squeamish about a few more killings, Herb told himself. He'd already crossed that line with Jane, and shooting these idiots had to be a helluva lot easier than smothering her had been. He wouldn't have to bury these bodies, either. Hell, this would be *much* easier than the ordeal he'd already endured. Besides, the early demise of Sid and Barry would be their own damned fault. What on earth had they been thinking about, kidnapping Jane Parkhurst Carmody right off the streets of Tiburon like that?

Fact was, Herb knew if he didn't take care of this thing right now, tonight—first, pick off his wife's kidnappers in "self-defense," then kill Ellen and make it look like Sid and Barry had done it and, finally, identify Ellen's dead body as Jane's—his own butt would be in the gas chamber in no time. Unless Kozlowski killed him first, of course—there was always that prospect to look forward to. Bottom line was, it was him or them—hell, this really *was* self-defense.

He'd still have the problem of Claire, of course, but Herb figured he'd have time to take care of his unwelcome houseguest after he'd finished up here. He'd call her as soon as he'd taken care of the three inside the house, lure her to some secluded spot nearby, kill her, and stuff her body in the trunk of her car. Make it look like a carjacking gone wrong. Chances were her body wouldn't be discovered for days. Other than proximity, there'd be nothing at all to tie her death to the others. She'd be just another tourist who'd ended up murdered.

If things worked out the way Herb planned, he figured he could kill Claire and still be back here to do his traumatized-husband act for the cops in under an hour. Then his only remaining task would be to erase every trace of the Merchant sisters' stay from his house.

He could do it. There was no real choice—he'd already bet his life on this game plan.

Herb made sure Sid and Barry were together in the living

room at the front of the house before he made his move. He did his best to remain calm, taking deep breaths the way he used to do before a big swim meet. He'd have to shoot accurately, that was for sure. Couldn't afford to ruin his self-defense story by merely wounding one of the kidnappers, or by being forced to shoot each of them three or four times to make sure they were dead.

It had been months since he'd gone to the shooting range and practiced. Yet his score hadn't been half bad that last time. He'd won his bet with Leo Smithers, hadn't he? And Leo was a Vietnam vet, trained by the U.S. Army. Besides, Herb always performed better when the pressure was on.

He gripped the gun tighter and banged on the door with his left fist.

There was a long pause, then a nervous-sounding Sid called out, "Who's there?"

"UPS. Delivery for Edwin Balzarian."

"What the—"

Herb heard a series of clicks as deadbolts were unlocked. As soon as the door opened, he shot Sid square in the chest at close range. The little man with the Elvis Presley haircut slumped to the ground, a puzzled expression forever chiseled onto his pudgy face.

Barry's over-muscled frame was lying on the sofa. As his smaller friend went down, the big man dove for one of the two handguns lying on the coffee table. Herb opened fire again. His first shot whizzed past Barry's head, but the second hit him in the left temple. Barry died sprawled across the coffee table, his own gun just a fraction of an inch out of reach.

Herb kicked the front door shut behind him and stepped over Sid's corpse and around the gore spread across the floor from the exit wound. The dead con artist's eyes were open and unfocused.

Barry was no longer breathing, either. *He'd done it,* Herb told himself, feeling a quick measure of relief. He'd felled them both without so much as a shot being returned. Of course, he would need proof of shots returned to make his story play out right.

Fighting off the repulsion he felt in touching Barry's still-warm body, Herb took the pistol from the table and pressed it into the dead man's limp hand. He fired a shot into the wall above the front door.

He repeated the same process with Sid and the second gun, this time firing into the cheap wallboard at the right of the front door. *There.* Now there was physical evidence that Herb had merely been returning fire from his wife's kidnappers. Too bad for them they were such lousy shots.

"I heard a shot inside the house, Officer," Herb rehearsed in his mind, "and I was terrified that the kidnappers had killed my wife. Frantic for her safety, I banged on the front door. When it opened, both kidnappers fired at me. I had no choice but to shoot them. It was just lucky they missed me, and that I came armed with my own gun."

Now to take care of Ellen. Herb slid his own weapon into the waistband of his pants and, using a handkerchief to keep from leaving fingerprints on it, headed upstairs with Sid's gun in his hand.

Ellen had been lying on the sofa in her room ever since she'd been returned to it. She'd been terrified when the kidnappers ordered her to put on that greasy old blindfold again and then hurried her down a flight of stairs. Were they planning to execute her? But all that happened was a phone call. Since they'd returned her to her room, she'd felt both relieved and tentatively hopeful that this nightmare might soon be over. After all, Herb Carmody had played along with the scam on the phone. He hadn't told the kidnappers they had the wrong woman. So maybe he would come up with the money to ransom her after all.

Now she bolted upright, terrified, when she heard a shot downstairs. Two more followed in rapid succession, then a pause before the fourth. Ellen heard a fifth shot fired downstairs. Then silence.

Her pulse pounded in her temples. Had the police come to rescue her? But, if so, who'd won the gun battle she'd just heard? What if her kidnappers had managed to shoot the cops instead of the other way around? If, indeed, there actually *were* any cops.

Her heart thumping wildly, Ellen leapt up and pressed her ear against the locked hallway door. She heard footsteps thundering up the stairs, heading toward her. Were they— whoever *they* were—coming to shoot her, too? She looked around frantically, but there was nowhere to hide in this sparse prison. She was a caged animal, at the mercy of whoever was heading her way.

The bathroom offered her only refuge, yet there was no way to lock the door. Her gaze fell upon the straight-back wooden chair. It might buy her a few minutes' time, she thought.

Ellen grabbed the chair and carried it into the bathroom. She pushed the door shut and angled the back of the chair under the door handle. Then she climbed into the tub, hoping its sturdy cast iron sides might stop a bullet. She curled into a fetal position and began to pray for her life.

As Claire crept through the shadows toward the yellow house, she saw Herb Carmody walk around the side of the house and stand for a moment opposite the front door. By the dim glow of the porch light, she could see he was holding a gun in his right hand. Worried he might spot her, she quickly darted behind a tree, peeking around it just in time to see Herb straighten up and begin to bang loudly on the door.

The instant the door opened, Herb opened fire on whoever was inside.

Claire heard three shots in rapid succession—were they all from Herb's gun? For a moment, she thought he was implementing some kind of plan to rescue Ellen. The front door slammed shut again. Two more gunshots followed, with significant delays between them. If this was a rescue mission, Claire began to think, it certainly was a very strange one.

She looked around, but no one emerged from either of the two lit-up houses across the road, or even appeared in the windows to peer out. With their doors and windows shut and, perhaps, their television sets or radios turned on as well, maybe they hadn't heard the gunfire, she thought. Or perhaps they had heard it and either were already calling the police or choosing not to become involved. Pulling her own weapon from her jacket pocket, she approached the yellow house.

Claire peeped through a side window of the living room and spotted the two dead men, one of them lying by the front door and the other prone across the coffee table. She didn't recognize either of them.

Herb was nowhere in sight. And where was Ellen? *Where the hell was Ellen?*

As quietly as she could, Claire sneaked around to the front of the house and tried the front door. It was unlocked. She pushed it open noiselessly, stepped around the smaller man's corpse, and listened for sounds elsewhere in the house. She closed her mind to the carnage surrounding her. This wasn't the first time she'd seen gunshot victims—during her days as a newspaper reporter, she'd covered a murder or two—but this time felt completely different. This wasn't somebody else's story, it was *hers. It was her family's.*

She stood still, listening intently for signs of life. Suddenly, at the back of the house, she heard heavy footsteps on the staircase. Her heart pounding and the little pearl-handled gun held ready to shoot if necessary, she headed toward the source of the noise.

Herb checked the two bedrooms closest to the top of the stairs and found them both empty. He headed down the hall toward the closed door at the end and quickly saw that someone had installed a cheap, keyless deadbolt lock on it. He snapped the bolt back and pushed the door open, entering the room with Sid's gun pointed straight ahead.

The room appeared to be empty. Herb jerked the sofa away from the wall, scraping it across the loose, soiled carpet. Ellen was not hiding there. He opened one of the sliding closet doors, but she wasn't cowering in that musty cubbyhole, either.

The room's only window was boarded shut, so she clearly hadn't escaped through it.

There was only one other place the woman could be. Herb tried the doorknob on what was probably a bathroom door. It swiveled in his hand, but when he pushed against the door, it didn't move. She must be standing on the other side, he thought, holding the door closed. He pushed again, using his shoulder and his full weight, but the door still didn't budge. Ellen had to be one strong woman.

Well, not for long. Herb took aim at one of the flimsy-looking door panels and fired a shot through it. The bullet pinged loudly against something inside the room. A radiator? A sink or toilet? Had the bullet gone clear through Ellen's body before hitting something more solid? There was no way of telling. He pushed against the door again.

Shit! It still didn't open. If he'd shot the bitch, why the hell hadn't she fallen to the floor? And if he'd missed her, surely she wouldn't have the nerve to keep standing there, pressing her body against a door his bullets could so easily penetrate.

He'd kick the door down, Herb decided. He backed up and took a run at it, using the sole of his shoe as a battering ram. *Fuck!* He felt the impact reverberate all the way to his teeth. But at least the door had splintered. A quick series of hammer blows against the damaged door with the gun barrel, and he was able to reach through it. His fingers gripped the chair back propped under the doorknob and slid it aside.

As the straight-back chair fell to the floor with a thump, Herb pushed the bathroom door open and stepped across the doorjamb.

Another gunshot ringing in her ears, Claire hurried up the stairs searching for Ellen. *Was she too late?* As she reached the upper floor of the house, she heard a loud smash, then a series of hammer blows, followed by the sounds of wood splintering and something falling to the floor. The noise seemed to be coming from the end of the hallway. She raced toward it.

Ellen knew she was about to die and, for the first time in her life, she honestly felt what her elderly patients must have experienced as they realized they had only hours, then minutes, then seconds left to live. No wonder they all wanted to make amends for their sins. But it wasn't cancer or heart disease or kidney failure that would kill her. It was some unknown man with a gun, shooting bullets through a bathroom door.

Her hopes of rescue rapidly withering, she cowered inside the cast iron bathtub, doing what little she could to wring every last second out of her life.

As Herb shoved open the bathroom door, Claire reached the end of the hallway. She saw him raise his gun and aim at something beyond the doorframe, out of her view. Was it Ellen?

"Hey!" she yelled, sinking into her shooting crouch, her gun aimed squarely at him with both hands steady. *"Herb!"*

The big blond man whirled around, a look of complete surprise on his handsome face. As he raised his gun and took aim in her direction, Claire fired one quick shot, hitting Herb in the center of his chest—precisely where that target-shooting instructor she'd once so resented had taught her to aim. Herb's gun went off as he fell backward, but his bullet was aimed high. It landed in the wall above her head.

Her ears ringing, Claire realized she was still alive and un-harmed.

Warily, her gun still pointed at him, she approached the fallen man. "Don't move, Carmody!" she ordered as his blood began to trickle across the floor. "Don't move or I'll shoot you again." She kicked the gun out of his loosened grip.

Herb made a brief gurgling sound and went silent. His eyes rolled back in his head.

"Claire! Thank God!"

Claire turned to see Ellen climbing out of an old-fashioned claw-foot bathtub. Her eyes went watery and her vision blurred. "Be careful," she warned her sister as she began to shake all over. "This guy is very dangerous. He was trying to kill you."

Ellen approached Herb and briefly placed two fingers on his neck, holding them against his carotid artery, as she'd done with so many of her patients. Then she stepped around him and circled her arms around her sister.

"He's not going to hurt anybody, ever again," she said gently, tears of relief now freely flowing down her own cheeks. "You saved my life."

Claire hugged her sister to her as hard as she could and began to sob.

The Merchant sisters clung to each other until their tears finally stopped. Then they walked downstairs together, found a telephone, and called the police.

16

"Just got the official word. You're free to leave town," attorney Lucy Gross told Ellen and Claire. Three days after the shootings, the three women were meeting in the young lawyer's sparsely furnished downtown Petaluma office.

"You mean both of us?" Ellen asked, sounding a bit suspicious. "I'm not going without Claire."

"Yes, both of you. Nobody's going to file charges. Didn't really expect they would, not under the circumstances, but you never know. Sometimes you can get an overzealous district attorney, some guy who figures he can get a conviction on carrying a concealed weapon or something."

Claire felt a rush of genuine relief. She'd been on pins and needles since the night of the shooting. The police had questioned her and Ellen separately for hours, obviously trying to find any small discrepancy in their stories. Finally, Claire, exhausted, had asked to see an attorney, and Lucy'd taken their case. Since then, the sisters had been staying in a cheap nearby motel. They'd continued to answer dozens of the cop's questions while Lucy did her best to protect their interests.

"It was a good thing Claire *was* carrying a concealed weapon," Ellen pointed out, "or we'd both be dead right now. But how'd you finally manage to get them to let us go, Lucy?" She included herself in her question only to show solidarity with Claire—she knew she'd done nothing illegal. But worrying that her sister might actually face prison time for saving her life had kept her awake nights.

"I'd like to tell you it was my superior legal abilities," Lucy continued with a smirk, "but the truth is, your stories simply added up. And then there were those tapes Claire made of the phone calls. They backed up your claims quite nicely."

"I'm not going to be prosecuted for illegal wiretapping or something, right?" Claire asked, visions of Linda Tripp dancing in her head.

"Not this time, but I wouldn't make a habit of it."

"That's one thing you don't have to worry about."

"Look, Claire, Ellen, both of you were obviously victims here, nothing more. It took the police so long to confirm that because this includes crimes committed in three different counties, and somebody had to pull together all the facts. Once they realized Jane Carmody was the Big Sur murder victim, and that she was the wife of the man Claire shot—"

"So Herb had already killed his wife before I even got off the plane?" Ellen asked, furrowing her brow. Piecing together dates from newspaper stories about the crime, she'd done the math.

"Best guess is that he killed her in Big Sur sometime on Saturday, the day before you arrived at SFO. A real estate agent recognized Carmody's photo after the kidnapping story hit the newspapers. She remembered renting him a cabin for that weekend and called the Monterey County Sheriff's office. They scoured the area around the cabin and found what looked like an empty shallow grave on the adjacent property. There were even a few scraps of the clothes Jane had been wearing mixed in with the disturbed dirt."

"But why bury his wife and then dig her up again and throw her off a cliff?" Claire asked, her brow furrowing. Had Carmody been completely crazy?

Lucy, a petite black-haired dynamo close to Ellen's age, perched with barely restrained energy on the edge of her leather executive chair. "The Monterey County deputies wondered the same thing, so they started looking around. Herb must have thought he'd buried his problems for good. Just not quite deep enough, as it turns out. Animals dug up Jane's body, and the owner of the property where Herb buried her found her corpse. Guy named Lester Klemp. Klemp and his brother-in-law were the ones who moved her to Hurricane Point."

"For god's sake, *why?*" Ellen asked, a look of sheer horror on her freckled face. She'd seen more than her share of dead people, and the last job she'd ever want to tackle was moving one, partially decomposed, out of a shallow grave. "Why didn't these guys just call the cops and report what they'd found?"

Lucy rolled her eyes as she told the sisters about the macabre situation. "Seems our Mr. Klemp didn't want to risk having the authorities find his cash crop—a very extensive marijuana patch. It was only a few hundred yards from Jane's grave."

"This whole thing is so incredibly bizarre," Ellen said. "I don't even see why on earth Herb would set up this house exchange thing in the—"

"Geez, Ellie, don't you get it?" Now it was Claire's turn to roll her eyes. "He set it up because he saw your photograph in that goddamned house exchange catalog and *you looked so much like his wife!*"

"But—"

"It wasn't your *house* he wanted," she explained with barely concealed impatience. "He wanted *you*. You were supposed to be his alibi—your being in that house was intended to make his neighbors think Jane was still alive and well at home while he was up in Seattle seeing artists."

"Claire's absolutely right," Lucy agreed.

"I still don't see how that would help him," Ellen insisted.

201

She hated feeling tricked. She'd been so proud of herself, scoring that Tiburon house for what she'd expected would be a luxurious free vacation. In the end, it had been briefly luxurious, but it had turned out to be anything *but* free. Or a vacation. It had turned into the single worst experience of her entire life.

Lucy chimed in with her theory. "The deal was, you were supposed to leave Jane's Jaguar back at the airport parking ramp when you went home to Minnesota, right?"

"Right," Ellen agreed.

"Chances are Herb would have reported his wife missing a day or two after he returned from Seattle. Thanks to you, her car would be found at the airport, with its parking record indicating it had been left there while he was probably out of town. If he got really lucky, somebody might even report that a red-haired woman matching his wife's description had parked it there and then gone into the airport. The cops would conclude Jane had left her husband of her own free will, and he'd be in fat city. Who'd ever know he was living high on *her* money? Anyway, that's my best guess."

"So, do you think the marriage went sour, or what?" Claire asked, thinking about her own marital troubles and the divorce negotiations that awaited her as soon as she returned to Santa Monica.

"Probably, but Herb had a bigger problem than a spat with Jane to contend with. The San Francisco cops put out feelers to a few of their informants and found out Herb owed at least a hundred grand in gambling debts. The sharks were descending."

"Let me guess," Claire said, recalling one of the calls she'd taped. She'd held back that recording, figuring it had nothing to do with the kidnapping. "He was in debt to a guy named Kozlowski."

Lucy's eyes widened. "How do you know that?"

Claire told her about the threatening phone call, during which Kozlowski'd assumed she was Mrs. Carmody. "But what I don't get is why Herb wouldn't just ask his wife for the money," she said. "Jane was loaded. She certainly could have afforded to bail him out if he was in that much trouble."

"All we can do is speculate about that," Lucy told them. "As you told me before, everything the Carmodys owned was in Jane's name, except for the art galleries, which they owned jointly. She must have had her reasons for keeping a very tight financial leash on her husband. Herb was from a fairly poverty-stricken background—his mother was a servant on an estate in Santa Barbara, not far from where Jane grew up in luxury. Santa Barbara's where the two of them met. Maybe she was afraid he'd married her for her money."

At least Claire knew Charlie hadn't married her for her money—she'd never had any. "I suppose, under those circumstances, Herb's asking Jane for a hundred thousand dollars to pay his gambling debts might have ended the marriage," she said. "Or maybe he simply knew she wouldn't give it to him."

"Either way, it certainly would cut off his access to the good life, which he seemed to enjoy a great deal," Lucy agreed. "So, instead of asking Jane for money, he killed her, used Ellen to create an alibi for himself, and undoubtedly figured he could siphon off his wife's inheritance while pretending to be a deserted husband."

"But how does all this fit in with my being kidnapped?" Ellen asked, still feeling confused.

Lucy shook her head. "We'll probably never know the whole truth about that," she admitted. "Sid Balzarian and Barry O'Farrell knew Herb, at least casually, from a San Francisco sports bar they all frequented. My best guess, after listening to those phone calls Claire taped, is that they cooked up the kidnapping scheme without Herb's knowledge. It was simply Ellen's bad luck they chose this particular time to implement it."

"I certainly seem to be having my share of bad luck lately," Ellen agreed with an audible sigh.

"But *you're* still alive, thanks to your sister here. That's a lot more than Jane Carmody and the others can say."

Ellen blushed. "Sorry, didn't mean to sound self-pitying."

"Look, you two, just go back home and try forget all about this, okay? Pretend it was all a bad nightmare. Take a nice vacation, maybe, and—"

"A nice vacation?" Claire asked, incredulous. "Lucy, this *was* our vacation." If she ever again had enough money to afford a vacation, she'd already decided to spend it on as many sessions of psychotherapy as she could afford. It was going to take her a long, long time to get over the experience of shooting a man to death, even if it was to save her sister's life.

"Sorry, wasn't thinking," Lucy said, glancing at her watch. "Hey, you'd better get going if Ellen's going to make her flight." She got up and ushered the sisters to the door.

Inside San Francisco International Airport, at the gate for the Minneapolis-St. Paul flight, Claire hugged Ellen goodbye. "I want you to promise me you'll never get mixed up in one of these crazy house exchange schemes again," she said.

Ellen shrugged.

"Ellie, I mean it!"

"Probably not," she agreed. "Unless it's a really, really great place and—"

"For god's sake, Ellen!"

"—*and* I make all the arrangements with the wife," she finished with an impish grin on her freckled face.

Claire couldn't really be angry with Ellen, not as she real-ized this was the first time her sister had actually smiled in days. "We'll talk about it first," she insisted. She hated sounding so much like a mother hen, yet she couldn't help feeling protective. That had been her role in the Merchant family since the day Ellen was born.

"So how about you, Claire? What are you planning to do for laughs?"

"Get back to work, I guess, try to scrape out a living. Get a divorce. My life's not exactly a laugh riot lately."

Ellen picked up her carry-on bag as the gate attendant opened the jetway door and began to collect passengers' boarding passes. "If you're going back to work right away, I have a suggestion for an article you could write," she said. "Or maybe it could even be a book."

"What's that?"

"A first-person kind of thing, an account of your personal experience with the vacation house exchange from hell."

"Are you serious?"

"Serious as snow," Ellen said, using a common phrase from their childhood. "You always told me one of the reasons you write is that it's sort of like therapy for you, right?"

"Yeah, I guess." Claire felt their roles suddenly were being reversed, that Ellen was now giving her advice. It felt a little strange, but not bad.

"So maybe writing about this nightmare would help you get over it, right? Anyway, think about it. Gotta go." Ellen planted another kiss on Claire's cheek and sprinted toward her plane. "Talk to you tomorrow," she called over her shoulder as she disappeared down the jetway.

Maybe Ellen's suggestion wasn't such a bad idea, Claire realized as she headed back toward the parking ramp. She certainly did need some therapy, some way to put this behind her. And, if she could manage to get past the personal horror she'd been through, she had to admit this was a pretty dramatic story. It had all the crucial elements of the best of the true crime genre.

By the time she'd reached her car and headed south on the freeway toward Santa Monica, Claire had already begun mentally composing the first paragraph of her new work.